Emily Harvale lives in East Sussex,
You can contact her via her websi
Instagram or Pinterest.

Author contacts:
www.emilyharvale.com
www.twitter.com/emilyharvale
www.facebook.com/emilyharvalewriter
www.facebook.com/emilyharvale
www.pinterest.com/emilyharvale
www.instagram.com/emilyharvale

***

Scan the code above to see all Emily's books on Amazon

Also by this author:

Highland Fling

Lizzie Marshall's Wedding

The Golf Widows' Club

Sailing Solo

Carole Singer's Christmas

Christmas Wishes – Two short stories

A Slippery Slope

The Perfect Christmas Plan – A novella

Be Mine – A novella

***

The Goldebury Bay series:

Book One – Ninety Days of Summer

Book Two – Ninety Steps to Summerhill

Book Three – Ninety Days to Christmas

***

The Hideaway Down series:

Book One – A Christmas Hideaway

Book Two – Catch A Falling Star

Book Three – Walking on Sunshine

Walking on Sunshine

Emily Harvale

ISBN 978-1-909917-16-3

Published by Crescent Gate Publishing

Print edition published worldwide 2016
E-edition published worldwide 2016

Editor Christina Harkness

Cover design by JR, Luke Brabants and Emily Harvale

In memory of Christina Hamilton Foster.
There are no words.

Acknowledgements

My special thanks go to the following:

Christina Harkness for editing this novel. Christina has the patience of a saint and her input is truly appreciated.

My webmaster and friend, David Cleworth who does so much more for me than website stuff.

Luke Brabants and JR for their work on the gorgeous cover. JR is a genius in graphic design and Luke's a talented artist. Luke's website is: http://www.lukebrabants.com

My fabulous friends for their support and friendship.

All of my Twitter and Facebook friends, and fans of my Facebook author page. It's great to chat with you. You help to keep me (relatively) sane!

To the members of my new Street Team. I love that you want to help promote my books and spread the word. You're the best!

And finally, you – for buying this book. Thank You. It really means a lot to me. I hope you enjoy it.

Walking
on
Sunshine

You simply need to take that step

Chapter One

Lucy clambered from the passenger seat of her best friend's beloved, sunshine-yellow Beetle and blinked several times. She stood open-mouthed on the dusty gravel parking area, completely lost for words.

'It's unbelievable, isn't it?' Beatrix beamed at Lucy and spread her arms wide as if she were attempting to hug the expansive vista stretched out before them.

Lucy half expected Beatrix to burst into a rendition of that opening song from 'The Sound of Music' and was thankful that she didn't. Beatrix and singing were not a happy combination. Lucy inhaled deeply and glanced at her friend.

'It certainly is.' Lucy wasn't lying. It *was* unbelievable. Just not in the way Beatrix had meant it.

'I knew you'd love it here as much as I do, once you saw it. Simply being here makes me feel so much more alive. This is what's really important in life. Breathing in fresh, clean, sea air, and having stunning views like this. It makes you realise just how incredible Mother Nature is.'

Lucy wasn't convinced. She could think of several things far more important in *her* life – and city air wasn't that bad. Neither was the view from her office on the sixteenth floor of the architect-designed twenty-seven-storey building in which she worked. She could see plenty of stunning sights reflected in the glass and polished metal of the skyscrapers surrounding the palatial offices of the international law firm of Cash, Roberts & Grieves.

And working in the litigation department of one of the top five legal practices in London was what was *really* incredible… and rather bemusing. Sometimes she expected to wake up and find it had all merely been a wonderful dream.

Beatrix grabbed their luggage from the boot and before Lucy could stop her, had unceremoniously dumped the cases on the dusty ground. There was no point in passing comment. No matter how many times Lucy told her friend otherwise, Beatrix considered all things equal and Lucy's prized Louis Vuitton suitcase deserved no preferential treatment as far as Beatrix was concerned.

Lucy looked away, pretending not to notice and scanned the seemingly never-ending open space. Fields, full of sheep and strewn with poppies and other wild flowers with names no doubt familiar to Beatrix, stretched out towards a canvas of sea and sky and, a horizon any artist would adore: all shades of pink, grey and indigo. Okay, the sunset was pretty spectacular, she would give Beatrix that. But as the final remnant of an orange sun faded like a deflating beach ball into the flat expanse of silver sea, Lucy already missed the bright lights of London.

Or any lights for that matter. With twilight fast encroaching, it was becoming apparent that it would soon be dark. Very dark. The last time she had spotted a street lamp was when they left Market Street – the main road through the village of Hideaway Down… That's if that narrow street, bordered either side by quaint, Olde Worlde shops, with an ancient Inn at one end and an equally time-trapped church at the other, could actually be called a main road.

Up here on Hideaway Cliff there wasn't a street lamp to be seen – or a light of any kind. Not one light. Nothing. Nada. Zilch. Not even the welcoming glow of a table lamp, emitting from the windows of the row of bijou, Victorian red-brick cottages, which were perched rather too close to the edge of the cliff for Lucy's liking. She could picture the sheer drop from here. It couldn't be more than half a mile away. How would people see it in the dark? Surely there must be some form of lighting? Was there even electricity in this back of beyond?

Panicking, Lucy pulled her phone from her Chanel handbag and checked for a signal. Thank Heaven for small mercies. There were three bars. Three glorious, life-affirming bars. She wasn't entirely cut off from the world... or more importantly, the office. But the signal appeared to fluctuate as she stared at it and she willed it to hold on to its tentative link to civilisation. For the first time in her life, she was even grateful that her phone contained a built-in torch; she'd clearly need it here.

Beatrix slammed the boot shut. 'Why are you frowning?'

Lucy met her friend's faltering smile and matched it. 'Sorry, Bea. I'm tired, that's all. It's... really something. Truly it is.' That was also the truth. It was something. Something out of Lucy's worst nightmare. She wouldn't be at all surprised to hear the stampeding paws of a suicide of lemmings (or whatever the collective name was for the furry little creatures) as they threw themselves off the cliff. She suspected she would be giving that idea some serious consideration herself after spending a few days here. It was probably the only way she could escape

3

the place.

Why, oh why, had she let Beatrix talk her into this? Lucy had only met Beatrix's, Aunt Petunia a couple of times when Aunty P, as Beatrix called her, had come to stay at the flat which Lucy and Beatrix shared. The flat belonged to Lucy, and Beatrix paid rent. When she could. Which wasn't often since she had moved in two years ago. Struggling actresses didn't earn much, apparently, whereas an ambitious young lawyer earnt enough to feed a small country – so Beatrix seemed to think, anyway.

Fortunately, Lucy did earn enough to feed herself and Beatrix. And to pay for most of the things Beatrix needed in her life. Well, that's what best friends do, right? And Beatrix would repay the favour ten-fold when she finally became a Hollywood star. Although quite how Beatrix planned to become such an icon without *actually* living in Hollywood – or without *actually* having any acting jobs scheduled on the day planner in the kitchen, was beyond Lucy's comprehension. But then most things Beatrix did were beyond Lucy's comprehension. Especially the men Beatrix dated. She shuddered at the thought of the last one. Then again, if Beatrix was still dating the loser, *he* would be here with her, and Lucy would be home in Greenwich. Where streetlights were plentiful.

Instead, Lucy had been invited to the wedding of Petunia Welsley and Bartram Battersfold which was to take place on Saturday the sixth of August at St Katherine's Church on Market Street in Hideaway Down at one p.m. Followed by a buffet at The Snowdrop Inn from two p.m. onwards and entertainment in Market Field at the August Fair from three p.m. till late. Dress code: Bright and colourful. Whatever that meant. Hats piled high with tropical fruits and dresses covered with large floral patterns, perhaps? Not the sort of wedding Lucy

4

would ever dream of having.

Hers would be a stylish affair. Wedding Breakfast at the magnificent Manorsfold Country House Hotel, near her parents' home in Berkshire – for close friends and family only. Wedding Ceremony at St Mary Magdalen Church, presided over by the Reverend Herbert Grimwald-Smythe. Lavish, five-course reception luncheon back at Manorsfold, followed by dancing in a marquee to music provided by a string quartet and a local band. Dress code: Formal. Men wearing morning suits; women wearing matching ensembles in tasteful colours. No children allowed.

Not that Lucy had given the matter much thought. Marriage was way down on her list of priorities.

She had also been invited by both Beatrix and Aunty P, to spend the week leading up to the wedding in one of the Gilroy's Happy Holiday Cottages on Hideaway Cliff: 'Cliff-top cottages with unrivalled 360 degree views of the sea; a quaint English village and countryside designated as an Area of Outstanding Natural Beauty', according to the website Beatrix showed her.

Lucy couldn't think of anything worse than spending a week in the country and when Beatrix told her about 'the warm and friendly villagers who'll know everything about you in ten minutes flat', Lucy knew she must have done something rather dreadful in a former life to deserve such punishment. Not that she believed in all that past lives stuff. That was Beatrix's thing. That and perfumed oils, hanging feathered chimes and scented soaps made from foraged plants. Lucy liked the scented soaps and it always amazed her that Beatrix could find so many suitable plants to forage… in Greenwich. But the rest of it – not so much.

Beatrix's smile returned. 'We're going to have a fabulous week. We're staying in Mistletoe Cottage. Did I tell you that it's named after the owner Janet Gilroy's, cat? Or the cat's named after the cottage. I'm not sure which.'

Lucy grinned. 'Seriously?'

Beatrix nodded. 'Yep. I suppose the cottage came first because it's old. Which makes sense because Holly and Ivy, Janet's twin daughters, were named after Holly Cottage and Ivy Cottage. I remember Aunty P telling me. And Merlot, Janet's Red Setter is named after Vine Cottage. Because Merlot's a grape… from a vine. Get it? And I've remembered...the cat's named after the cottage.'

'I'm so glad we cleared that up. Um…when you said these cottages were just outside the village, I thought you meant a few metres, not over a mile up a steep hill and balancing on a cliff edge. We're not going to have to use candles, are we? And cook our meals over an open fire or something? Because I'm telling you now, Beatrix Welsley, as much as I love you, I'm leaving you here and going to a hotel, if that's the case. I don't do rural. You know that.'

Beatrix giggled. 'Hardly on the cliff edge. They're at least 1000 metres away, and yes, there's electricity. And a Rayburn…but that's solid fuel, so you'd best leave the cooking to me.'

'Phew. You don't know how relieved I am to hear that. Especially the electricity part. I was thankful that my phone's got a torch, and then I started wondering how I'd charge my phone. I could feel the palpitations starting.' Lucy glanced around. 'How do people move around up here at night? I can imagine this place gets as dark as a bat's bum once the twilight disappears.' She had seen the moon earlier but there was no sign of it now. It was obviously obscured by the dark clouds that had rolled across the sky during the journey down here. Lucy would have seen that as an omen if she believed in such things, which of course she didn't.

'They use a torch to see the way to their cars and then they drive down to the village. Or call a minicab.'

'There's a minicab?' Lucy pictured a horse and cart, but that was ludicrous. She'd seen at least two other cars as Beatrix had turned off Hideaway Lane or whatever it was called, and driven first one way through the village, turned around outside The Snowdrop Inn and driven back, so that Lucy "could see the full length of Market Street". Although... she'd also spotted a blacksmith's sign hanging motionless in the still evening air as Beatrix did the U-turn outside the pub – the only pub apparently. So there must be horses somewhere hereabouts.

'Yes. Brian's minicab. But he gets most of his fares from Eastbourne, which is a few miles away in that direction.' Beatrix pointed to a cluster of lights in the distance. 'Eastbourne's quite a large town.'

'Can't we stay in Eastbourne? Pretty please.'

Beatrix grinned. 'No. We can't. Let's dump our stuff inside and head to the pub. Aunty P and Bartram will be there. I can't wait to see them. And you can meet some of the villagers. It'll soon be closing time and you clearly need a glass of wine.' Beatrix grabbed her bags and one of Lucy's, and strode towards the door of Mistletoe Cottage.

'A bottle, more like.' Lucy pressed the number for her office, on her phone. 'Just giving Nikki a quick call and I'll be right behind you.'

Beatrix glanced back, tutted and shook her head. 'Can't you forget about work for one evening?' She clearly didn't expect a reply. Retrieving a key from beneath a potted geranium, she let herself in to Mistletoe Cottage.

'Cash robbers and thieves. Lucy Draycourt's office. How may I help you?'

Lucy grinned. Since the day her personal assistant,

Nikki, had joined the law firm of Cash, Roberts & Grieves, Nikki had referred to it as cash robbers and thieves whenever she was speaking to Lucy. As a junior associate, Lucy should have told Nikki in no uncertain terms not to defame the firm, but as ambitious as she was, Lucy had a sense of humour. Besides, she knew how the 'time costing' worked – and Nikki wasn't too far from the truth.

'One day, Nikki, I'm going to lend my phone to a senior partner and let him hear how you malign such a prestigious law firm. You'll find yourself on the receiving end of a defamation suit.'

'Yeah, yeah. So what's it like in the Sussex countryside? Do the locals all have three eyes and say things like "Ooo-ah"? Has the heel of your Manolo Blahniks stepped into a stinky cow-pat? Are you having fun-fun-fun?'

'Only pirates – and possibly those from the West Country say "Ooo-ah". I haven't met any locals yet. I flicked threw a copy of Country Life when I was at the dentist last week and sensibly purchased a pair of Hunter wellies and, even if I could see – which I can't because it's getting dark and they can't afford street lights, it seems – I don't think there is any fun-fun-fun to be had in Hideaway Down. Even lemmings avoid the place. Please tell me there's an emergency and the partners have insisted I return immediately.'

'Sorry. No can do. And why are you calling me at the office at nine-thirty on a Friday evening? Don't you know that, unlike you, I have a life outside of these hallowed walls?'

'Which is why I knew you'd still be there. It's month-end drinks night.' Lucy wished she hadn't had to miss out on that. Month-end drinks had been something Henry, the

8

senior partner of the litigation department, had started about six months ago, "... to keep the troops happy," he'd said. It was a way for the whole department to get together and discuss any problems. He felt it helped to break down barriers between the fee earners and the support staff; and helped everyone see that long hours and dedication brought additional rewards.

Lucy wasn't sure free food and wine were really the sort of additional rewards most people wanted, but the drinks nights had certainly helped to break down some barriers – and not just between the fee earners and the support staff. Last month had broken down a barrier between her and Henry. He'd kissed her in the lift as they were leaving. Sadly for her, the lift stopped on the fourth floor, and so did the kiss. William Peterson, the senior partner of the commercial conveyancing department got in and promptly engaged Henry in a discussion about a mutual client.

When they reached the ground floor lobby, Henry had scuttled off with William without so much as a backward glance at Lucy. Since then, Henry had behaved as if the kiss hadn't happened and Lucy had almost begun to wonder if it actually had. But she must not think about Henry or what might have happened if she could have been there on this drinks night.

'Oh yeah. That had completely slipped my mind.' Nikki let out a laugh. 'You know me. Anything for a free glass of wine. Especially the expensive stuff this lot supply. I keep telling you, the forty-odd-thousand pounds a year these misers pay me isn't even enough to feed a cat – if I had one – which I don't due to the fact that I can't afford to feed one. What colour Hunters did you buy? Or do they only come in green? And why didn't you show them to me?'

'Because they only arrived today. Beatrix had to get up and sign for them, so she wasn't best pleased. They come in a variety of colours. Naturally, I chose black. With a raised front and a back strap. They're very posh, don't you know. And oddly enough, rather sexy in a Jilly Cooper novel, sort of way.'

'Ooh-ah. I can picture you now, romping in a haystack with a muscle-bound, shirtless, yokel, your black hair matted with straw.'

'P...lease. Apart from the fact that I haven't even seen one haystack, you wouldn't find me near one, let alone having sex in it. And you know I don't have time for men... other than Henry. I've got a glass ceiling to break through. Are you sure he doesn't need me to abandon this holiday and come back?'

'Afraid not. Do you want me to tell everyone you've gone somewhere exotic? A week in St Tropez would probably impress the gods of the twenty-seventh floor a lot more than seven days in an unknown village by the English Channel.'

'Too late. I told Henry I was going to a cottage in East Sussex. Although I'm not sure he actually heard me. In fact, I'm not convinced he'll even notice I'm not there. It doesn't do much for my ego to know that he seems to have no interest in what I do, or where I am, until he needs me to do something.'

It wasn't just Henry, either – although it would have been nice to think he cared, especially after that kiss. But even human resources hadn't appeared in the least bit interested in Lucy's holiday. She'd personally handed in the form, joking that she hoped it was the right one because it had been so long since she'd taken a holiday that the forms may well have changed. Tabitha, one of several assistants in Personnel, merely shrugged and took

10

the form, placing it on a pile of papers on her desk without looking at it. Cash, Roberts & Grieves had a staff of over one thousand in the London office alone, and Lucy was one of twenty junior associates, so she shouldn't be surprised. Except she was. And just a little disappointed. Especially about Henry's lack of interest.

She'd had a bit of a hero-worship vibe for Henry long before that kiss. Probably from the minute she'd seen him, and that was more than five years ago when she'd joined the firm shortly after her twenty-fourth birthday. Since then she'd come to like him even more. She wasn't quite in love with him but she was pretty damn close, especially after that stolen moment in the lift. Henry was a junior partner in litigation when she started work there and it had taken him about a year to remember her name, but in spite of that, she had risen faster than any other woman in the firm and she was certain that was partly due to Henry's influence. She was sure she'd make associate soon and then junior partner, followed by partner and then, like Henry was now, senior partner of a department.

One day, if she worked really hard and brought in enough high-revenue clients, she might even be the first woman to ever be given an office on the twenty-seventh floor – the floor reserved for executive partners. The floor where all the power – and money – mingled. Cash, Roberts & Grieves' very own Heaven. And by then, she might even be married to Henry, or at the very least, living with him.

She had her future all worked out. Although once or twice lately, she had woken up in the middle of the night and wondered if this was really what she wanted. Beatrix had told her she needed time out. "Time to find yourself," Beatrix had said even though Lucy told her she wasn't lost. She was simply anxious about the future and that was normal, wasn't it? Didn't everyone sometimes feel that life seemed to be in control of them instead of them being in control of their lives? Everyone had doubts, didn't they? Everyone had questions.

Lucy would rather like to know why Henry had kissed her and then treated her as if she were no different to anyone else in the firm. She'd like to be brave enough to ask him. But she wasn't. She didn't want to do or say anything that might put her glowing future in jeopardy.

'At least he knows your name,' Nikki said, sighing. 'The other day he called me Becky.'

'He's a very busy... What was that?' Lucy held the phone a fraction away from her ear and peered into the semi-darkness, straining to hear the sound she'd caught in the still night air surrounding her.

'What? I didn't hear anything. Lucy? Are you still there?'

'Shush. Yes I'm here... but... there's something on the other side of the bushes. It seems to be running.'

'It's probably a horse. Or a cow.'

'Do cows run?'

'I think so. Perhaps you should be the one running. It could be a bull.'

'A bull? Oh. My. God!'

'I can't hear you running, Lucy.'

'Because I'm not. You're not supposed to run.' Lucy's fingers tightened around her phone. 'They chase you.'

'That's bears.'

'You think it's a bear!'

Nikki tutted. 'Don't be ridiculous. There aren't any bears in Sussex. I meant it's bears you shouldn't run from. Bulls, you most definitely should. And as fast as your new Hunter wellies will let you.'

'I think I'm safe. There's a hedge between me and it.'

'Bulls are strong. It might be able to get through a hedge. I like working for you and I don't want to look for another job because you've been gored to death by a bull. Run, Lucy!'

'It's... it's... snorting. And panting. It's... Oh shit! There's a gap in the hedge and...' Lucy turned to run. 'Arghh!'

A solid mass burst through the gap and careered into her. She tumbled to the ground, the force of the impact knocking the air from her lungs, as first her arm, then her body thumped against grass, wild flowers and concrete-hard earth. It was as if a thousand tiny needles had shot into her. Had she landed amongst a swarm of bees? That would be nothing compared to what was to come. Lucy closed her eyes, certain that at any second she would be impaled on a pair of large horns and tossed in the air by the bull – like a red rag.

'What the...?' a deep voice asked, in a shocked tone, from right beside her.

Bulls can't speak. Lucy opened her eyes and looked in that direction. This was no bull. Although his nostrils flared, his face – a deep shade of crimson – was definitely human. But his startlingly blue eyes pierced right through her as soundly as any bull's horns ever could.

He gasped for breath, mumbled a curse which Lucy couldn't quite make out, and sprang to his feet.

'You okay?' he asked, with evident concern. 'Here, let me help you up.'

'Ow! Ow! Ow!' The bees were still stinging. Except there were no bees. A flattened patch of nettles was wreaking revenge on her bare arms. She reached for the man's hand and scrambled to her feet. 'No! I'm not okay. Why the hell don't you look where you're going? You must've heard me talking. Surely you could've avoided

13

me.'

'What?' He yanked earbuds from his ears, pulled his phone from the pocket of his shorts and pressed the screen. 'Sorry, I was listening to music. Didn't hear a thing. What did you say?'

'I said…'

Wow! Those eyes were even more startling, up close. And his mouth… Gosh! He was handsome. And oddly enough, he was built like a bull – all solid muscle with broad shoulders, an iron-hard grip, firm jaw… kissable lips… eyes you could drown in.

His brows furrowed. 'Are you in shock? Your eyes look glazed. Are you okay?'

'Huh?' was all she could manage as she stared at him.

'Lucy!'

Beatrix raced down the path from Mistletoe Cottage, the beam from the torch on her phone momentarily blinding Lucy in the semi-darkness. Typical Beatrix. Always trying to help. Always bad timing.

Lucy pulled herself together, dragged her gaze from the stranger, and brushed herself down. 'I'm okay, Bea. Just had the wind knocked out of me, that's all. And been stung by ten thousand nettles.'

'My fault,' the man said graciously. 'I was running and I didn't see you. Sorry.' His eyes again met Lucy's. 'I don't think there's any real damage but I'd like to take a look.'

'Are you a doctor?' Things were looking up.

He shook his head and a lock of blond hair fell into his eyes. He shoved it back and grinned. 'No. But I do know a thing or two about injuries. I used to be a physiotherapist for a premier-league football team.'

'Really? My PA would love you. She's heavily into football. Oh! Where's my phone? I was talking to her

14

when you knocked me flying.'

The three of them searched the long grass, Beatrix and the man using their phone torches.

'I've found it.' The man held Lucy's phone in the air a few feet away. 'And I'm guessing this is yours too.' He was clutching her Chanel handbag in his other hand as he walked back towards her.

'Thanks.' She took the bag and phone and, on hearing Nikki's voice, raised the phone to her ear. 'You're still there! Hi, Nikki. It's okay. It wasn't a bull.'

'Bloody hell, Lucy! You frightened the life out of me. Er. Was that a man's voice I heard?'

'Uh-huh.'

'Ooh-ah! What's he like?'

'I can't really say right now.' Lucy smiled at the man and glanced at Beatrix.

'From the soft, lilting tone you've suddenly adopted, I'm guessing he's pretty hot.'

'Yes, that's right. I'd better go. My assailant...' Lucy grinned and again glanced at the man. 'Sorry, I don't know your name.'

He grinned back. 'Evan. Evan Foster.'

'Hi Evan. I'm Lucy Draycourt.'

'And I'm Nikki, her long-suffering PA,' Nikki yelled.

Lucy coughed lightly into her phone. 'Evan's going to take a look at me to check I'm okay, so there's no need to worry. I'll call you during the week.'

'You'd better. I want to hear all about this guy. For someone who, less than five minutes ago, didn't have time for men, you've suddenly changed your tune. You'll be hunting for haystacks next.'

'Well, what can I tell you? I need to let... Evan check me over. I am on holiday, after all, and I mustn't let anything ruin that. Have a great evening.' Lucy pressed

15

end, dropped her phone in her bag and, with her best smile in place, met Evan's questioning look. 'Work,' she said, turning towards the cottages. 'Some people would think I don't have a life outside of the office. Oh, this is my best friend, Beatrix. We're staying in one of these cottages. Do you live around here?'

'Hi, Beatrix.' Evan smiled and nodded before returning his gaze to Lucy. 'No. I'm also here on holiday. And to attend my uncle's wedding. I arrived this evening.'

'No way!' Beatrix said. 'D'you mean Bartram Battersfold? Is he your uncle? He's marrying my aunt. Wow! What're the chances of that?'

Evan's eyes opened wide. 'You're kidding. What a small world.'

'It's a small village,' Lucy said.

'Huh?' Evan frowned. 'Oh, I see. Of course. Let's get you inside so that I can make sure you're okay.'

'She's okay,' Beatrix said, smiling. 'In fact I think she's feeling better than she's felt for a very long time. Aren't you, Lucy?'

Lucy met Beatrix's mocking look. 'It must be the sea air. Although… I do feel a little light-headed.'

Evan was beside her in a split second and wrapped an arm around her waist. 'Let me help you. You can never be too careful after a fall like that. And you landed in those nettles. We need to soothe the stings with vinegar, or witch hazel if you have any.'

'I've got tea-tree oil,' Beatrix said. 'That's even better.'

Evan smiled. 'That's perfect.'

'Whatever you say,' Lucy said, leaning into him. He was pretty damn perfect himself. But if this new tingling sensation was caused by the nettles, she didn't think she needed treatment. It was surprisingly rather nice.

16

Chapter Two

Evan closed the door of Ivy Cottage and cursed his stupidity. Why had he got himself involved? He could have simply apologised for knocking... what had she said her name was? Linda? No, Lucy. For knocking Lucy flat on her back and nearly landing on top of her. After all, it wasn't even entirely his fault. Why was she standing in front of the gap in the hedge in the first place? And surely she had heard him coming? She could have moved out of his way and then he wouldn't have careered into her. But he had. Even so, he should have simply apologised, helped her to her feet, and moved on. Why had he offered to check her over?

He shook his head and a fragment of a smile tugged at the corner of his mouth. He knew the answer to that. Because she was rather attractive. Many men would have probably found her stunning. All flowing, glossy black hair, slim body, long legs and eyes the colour of molten gold sprinkled with brown flecks. As if someone had shaken a dusting of cocoa powder in them.

That made the smile vanish. That was the sort of thing Diana would have said. And Diana was the last person he wanted to think about right now. But from the minute he'd arrived in Hideaway Down he'd done nothing except think about her. And talk about her with his aunt Beth and his uncle Bartram and later, with Bartram's soon-to-be-wife, Petunia. He hadn't meant to but they had asked him how he was and that inevitably led on to whether he was over the 'whole Diana nightmare', as Bartram had always referred to it and continued to do so now. Beth had even asked how he felt about staying at the cottages, 'after everything that happened'. Evan hadn't been sure whether he wanted to laugh... or cry. Except grown men didn't shed tears over women, so his father often said. And his dad should know. Greg Foster had had several dozen since Evan's mum had died thirty years ago.

'People you love either die, or they leave you, or you stop loving them and you leave. Either way, it's not worth crying about. Not after the first time, anyway,' Evan's dad had told him, many years later. But Aunt Beth and Uncle Bartram had said that Greg was a wreck after losing Evan's mum, and Greg may have had several dozen women but he never married again. Not after Chrissie. Because Chrissie Battersfold-Foster was the love of Greg Foster's life.

Just like Evan was convinced that Diana was the love of his.

Diana adored Hideaway Down and the cutesy, Gilroy's Happy Holiday Cottages. Evan had brought her here several times and, two and a half years ago, he had proposed to her at the very edge of Hideaway Cliff on a particularly blustery New Year's Eve. She had been so surprised that for a moment she had simply stared, open-mouthed, at him and the ring he was holding out to her in a velvet box. All the while, he knelt on frost-covered grass, the cold seeping into his bones, holding his breath, waiting for her answer.

Eventually she had said, 'Yes', and afterwards they had returned to Vine Cottage – the one in which they were staying – opened the bottle of champagne he had secretly placed in the fridge earlier, toasted to their future in front of a roaring log fire, and made love all night. It was one of the most romantic times of his life.

He looked around the interior of Ivy Cottage and sighed. It was similar to Vine Cottage in many ways and yet so different in its décor and furnishings. Vine had a more contemporary design; Ivy had a vintage theme. But both were perfect for a romantic getaway. In fact, all three cottages available to rent were perfect. Only one, Holly Cottage had permanent residents: the owner's daughter, Holly Gilroy who ran The Book Orchard, the new bookshop in the village, and her boyfriend, the author, Gabriel Mann.

But Evan wasn't here for romance. Well, not his in any event. He was here for his uncle's wedding, and to try to come to terms with the fact that a little over six months after Diana had said she would marry him, she had run off with his business partner, Darren, and she wasn't coming back anytime soon.

Wasn't coming back at all.

Ever.

And he must keep reminding himself of that fact. It was the only way he had any hope of moving on.

'At least she only took her half of the joint account money,' Bartram had repeated earlier today when Evan, Evan's aunt Beth and he were discussing the situation for the umpteenth time since Diana had left Evan, two years ago this week. 'She could've taken more. Thank your lucky stars for that, my boy.'

Beth, Bartram's older sister, nodded in agreement. 'And as I've said all along, you're better off without her.'

Bartram frowned. 'As for that Darren, I knew he was a wrong-un the moment I laid eyes on him. I should have said as much at the time and warned you not to go into business with him but I've been wrong about people before, and I hoped I was wrong about him. Some friend he turned out to be, running off with your fiancée like that. But you take after your darling mother. Always wanting to see the best in people, just like sweet Chrissie did.'

Beth nodded again. 'And always willing to forgive, no matter what hurt someone has caused. Just like darling Chrissie. Rest her dear soul.'

Bartram took his sister's hand and squeezed it. 'I wish she could be here with us now.' He smiled at Evan, his rheumy eyes even more watery than they had been. 'Your mum told me many years ago that I'd know the moment I met the love of my life, just as she knew when she met your father. And she was right. I fell in love with my Petunia the minute I saw her and I knew she was the one for me. But I didn't believe I had a hope of her returning my feelings. You could've knocked me down with a feather when she said she did. Chrissie would have loved her almost as much as I do, I'm sure of that. And you know, my boy, one day you'll meet the love of your life, too. And she won't be called Diana. Mark my words.'

'She may be,' Beth said with reason. 'But she won't be *that* Diana.'

'There'll never be another Diana,' Evan said. 'And she *was* the love of my life.'

'Nonsense,' Beth snapped. 'If she was she'd be here with you now, instead of gallivanting off, who knows where with your former best friend. No, no. You haven't met the one for you yet. But she's out there somewhere, Evan and one day in the not too distant future, your uncle Bartram and his new wife, Petunia, me and my darling

Henry, will be at your wedding. Take my word for it.'

He knew his aunt and uncle meant well, and he knew they still loved his mother, their baby sister, even though she had died of cancer thirty years ago when Evan was only two years old. But they could never seem to understand how he felt about Diana. Or what her leaving had done to him. The fact that she had left with his business partner and best friend had made it all the more difficult to deal with, only adding to the pain and loss he felt. But Beth and Bartram were right; he would forgive her tomorrow if she came back. He'd forgive Darren too – although maybe not quite so quickly.

The simple fact was, he still loved Diana. Still missed her as if she'd only left a week ago and would be coming home any day now. Still yearned to hold her in his arms; to kiss her and make love with her. To laugh with her. To make plans with her. Was that so wrong?

He knew the answer to that question, too. She wasn't coming back. He had to move on. He had to make plans for his own future. A future without Diana. The business had moved on, he'd seen to that. And Darren may have run off with Diana but at least he had only taken his share of the business profits and he'd had the decency to sign over all his rights to the business, to Evan. That was something.

Diana had frequently complained that all Evan did was work. Well, that was certainly all he had done since she had left him. He may have lost Diana but he had made damn sure he would not lose the business and it was in better shape now than it had ever been. He had changed its name to Foster Fitness which now ran training programmes, health and well-being courses, and weight-loss boot camps from ten bases scattered across the UK. Evan had managers in place at each one and had spent most of the past few months building up the online shopping site for Foster Fitness sports clothing, equipment and accessories. His love life may be bleak, his personal life a complete mess, but his work life was reaching peaks that he had never dared to imagine.

It was almost ironic. Now that he was in a position to step back from the day-to-day running of the business and spend more time on his personal life, he had no one to spend time with. He had friends of course, although not that many outside of the fitness world, but he did not have anyone special. He did not have Diana. If he could swap everything he had now, in return for Diana, he would do so in a heartbeat.

Beth had said there was someone out there for him but he couldn't see it. He could not imagine being in love with anyone other than Diana. Couldn't conceive of wanting to make love with someone else. Didn't even particularly want to kiss another woman, no matter how attractive she may be.

Take just now for example and Lily – no, Lucy. She was stunning. He could not help but see that. But when he had checked her over after her fall, had he wanted to touch her other than in a professional manner to ensure there were no broken bones? No, he hadn't. He had noticed that her skin was as soft as the new range of faux-silk robes his business provided in the massage waiting areas, but that was all. Had he wanted to kiss her when she'd leant towards him and parted her lips provocatively? No, not for one moment, even though he could see why many men would. Had lust coursed through him when she had asked him to feel if there was a bump on her head, and he'd traced his hands through her lustrous, waist length black hair to check that there wasn't? No. He'd simply realised how easy it would be to get his hands entangled in those dark locks and had taken care not to catch his watch strap.

Beth and Bartram may want him to believe that he would find someone new but it was all too clear to him that he wasn't over Diana and he wasn't likely to be for a very, very long time. It was over two years since she'd left and he was no nearer replacing her now than he was then. Not that she could be replaced. He knew that.

He'd seen the look in Lucy's radiant eyes. He didn't know much about women – Diana had proved that – but he did know when a woman was flirting with him. And Lucy had definitely been flirting. Perhaps she was looking for a holiday fling. Perhaps she just liked the look of him. People were always telling him that he was a handsome guy even though he couldn't see it himself – and Diana had clearly thought he wasn't as handsome as Darren. Perhaps Lucy merely flirted with every guy she met. He had no idea. But why, oh why had he agreed to go with her and Beatrix to the pub? That was just plain stupid.

He didn't want company; he wanted to be alone. To soak in a long bath, with a glass of whisky in one hand and a good book in the other. He wanted an early night. He'd travelled down from Oxford this morning in heavy traffic. He'd spent the afternoon with Beth and Bartram in The Coffee Hideaway, eating cake and drinking more tea than he had done for months. Petunia and Bartram had taken him to The Snowdrop Inn for an early dinner, again with Beth but also with her husband, Henry and their son Harry, Evan's cousin.

Evan had already seen most of the villagers and caught up with everyone's lives, enduring more questions about his own than he had found comfortable. He had finally managed to make his escape by saying he needed to go for a run and to have an early night – both of which had been true. Now he was going to have to go back down and face them all again… with two women he had only just met. He could imagine what the villagers would make of that.

He groaned loudly. Knowing his luck, Beth would think she'd foreseen his future and that he was interested in one of the women. And what was it that Petunia, his soon-to-be-aunt had said?

"You can't see the sun if you're staring into clouds, but sometimes all you need to do is take a step in a different direction and you'll be walking on sunshine."

Whatever the hell that meant. And surely it should be walking *in* sunshine, not *on* it? Although wasn't there a song about walking on sunshine, or a film, or something? He couldn't recall. Perhaps it meant his future would be filled with light and happiness. Petunia was into all that new-age philosophy gubbins, so it probably meant something profound that had gone right over his head. All he knew for sure was that it had something to do with finding romance.

Not that it mattered. As far as his love life was concerned he wouldn't be walking on sunshine, in sunshine, or anywhere near sunshine unless a certain blonde, blue-eyed, yoga-teaching, goddess, turned up in Hideaway Down and said she'd made the biggest mistake of her life – and asked him to take her back.

Which he would.

Without hesitating for a second.

Chapter Three

The interior of The Snowdrop Inn was exactly as Lucy imagined it would be. Two large fireplaces, dormant in this summer heatwave, dominated each end of a long, low ceilinged, room with a bar running almost its entire length. There were comfy armchairs scattered among tables and chairs, nearly all of which were occupied by customers chatting animatedly, or chortling with laughter over some shared joke, perhaps.

Lucy was surprised at the number of people sitting at the tables outside and lolling on the grass bank leading from the pavement to the blackened oak, pub door. Surely they couldn't all be residents of Hideaway Down or even holidaymakers staying at the cottages or other establishments in the village?

'No,' Evan said. 'People come here from miles around. It's a very popular pub, no matter what the season.'

Lucy hadn't realised she had voiced her question, so was taken aback by Evan's reply. All she said was: 'Oh.'

'There's Janet Gilroy.' Beatrix pointed to a friendly-looking, middle-aged woman behind the bar who was laughing with two auburn haired women. 'And I recognise Holly and Ivy Gilroy from their laughs as well as their hair, even from the back. Hello everyone.' She waved as the two women turned around and smiled, along with Janet.

'Beatrix? Is that really you?' Janet asked. 'You've changed your hair colour since I last saw you. When was that? February? March?'

'April.'

'Really?' Ivy said. 'Was it only April? It feels like we haven't seen you for… well, months and months. Come over here and give us all a hug.'

Beatrix laughed and did as Ivy requested, saying: 'Yes, Janet. It's really me. I got tired of having boring old plain brown hair. I wanted to try something more… distinctive.'

'Well, you've certainly done that, dear. Ginger suits you – and there's something I never thought I'd hear myself say. But it really does.'

'Thank you. I like it. It was Lucy's idea. Oh. You don't know Lucy, do you? Lucy, meet Janet, Holly and Ivy. Oh, and do you all know Evan. He's—'

'We know Evan,' Holly interrupted, smiling at Lucy. 'And besides, he was in here earlier with his family, weren't you, Evan?'

'And I thought you said you wanted an early night?' Ivy added.

'I did.'

Evan looked sheepish and Lucy wondered why.

'Until he met us,' Beatrix said, grinning. 'He knocked Lucy flying. Literally. He came bounding out from a hedge and knocked her flat on her back.'

Ivy laughed, but then seemed to wish she hadn't. 'Are you okay, Lucy?' she asked through fingers stifling her giggle.

'I'm fine, thanks. Although I did get stung by a bunch of nettles, but Beatrix has drowned me in tea-tree oil so I can't feel a thing, and Evan kindly checked me over to make sure I hadn't broken anything.'

'Oh, Evan,' Ivy said, winking at him. 'Is that what you do when you want to check a girl out? Knock her flying.'

'I didn't do it on purpose.' He sounded upset. And rather defensive.

'I enjoyed it anyway,' Lucy added, suddenly regretting the remark as all eyes turned to gaze at her.

'I don't blame you,' Ivy said. 'If I wasn't madly in love with my boyfriend, Ned, I'd loiter by a hedge and make sure Evan knocked me flat on my back too.'

'I wasn't loit... oh, you were teasing.'

Ivy nudged Lucy in the side. 'And you'd better get used to it. We're all a bit mad in Hideaway Down.'

'You speak for yourself,' Holly said. 'Where is Ned, by the way? I haven't seen him all evening.'

'He's at his mum's.' Ivy sauntered around the bar and refilled her glass of wine. 'Audrey needed some shelves put up or something and we all know how much I like avoiding getting roped in where there's work to be done. He'll meet me here when he's finished. Wine anyone?' She held the bottle up to offer it to Lucy and the others.

Lucy shook her head. 'Not for me. I'd rather have a gin and tonic, please.'

'Coming up,' Janet said, moving towards the optics. 'Southern Comfort for you, Beatrix?'

Beatrix nodded. 'Yes please.'

'I'll get it,' Ivy offered. 'Evan? Another whisky?'

He seemed unsure but shrugged and nodded. 'Why not. I am on holiday I suppose and we walked here across the fields, so I don't have to worry about driving.'

'Yes,' Lucy said. 'That was... delightful. I'm so glad Beatrix suggested that.'

'Then I'll make it a double,' Ivy said. 'And Mum, I

think Lucy needs a double G&T, by the sound of it. Walking not one of your favourite pastimes, Lucy?'

'Er. No. Not really. And certainly not in the country, across fields, in the pitch black.'

Beatrix tutted. 'It wasn't pitch black. We could see where we were going. Just. Mind you, it will be pitch black on the way home.'

'Wonderful.' Lucy glanced at Janet. 'I couldn't have the whole bottle, could I? With a straw.'

'I hope you're not afraid of bats,' Ivy said as Janet passed Lucy a very large drink.

'Bats?' Lucy hadn't meant to shriek. 'No one mentioned there'd be bats. I hate bats.'

'Have you actually seen a bat?' Evan asked, taking the glass Ivy handed him. 'They're not as bad as you might think.'

'They fly into your hair. That's all I need to know.'

'That's a myth,' Evan assured her. 'Well, they wouldn't do it on purpose but they might if their sonar wasn't working properly and—'

'Please! Can we not talk about bats!' Lucy shivered and took three large gulps of her drink. She wasn't joking about wanting the bottle. God only knew what other creatures were lurking in the darkness out there. As if bats weren't bad enough.

'Are Aunty P and Bartram still here?' Beatrix asked, changing the subject. 'I said I'd pop in and meet them for a drink if we arrived in time. The traffic was awful so we only arrived around nine-thirty, and then of course, Lucy got knocked over, so there was a bit of a delay.'

'Sorry about that,' Lucy said.

'It was my fault,' Evan added.

Beatrix frowned. 'I wasn't laying blame. I was simply explaining why we didn't get here until now, that's all. I suppose Aunty P's gone home to bed. I know she's not one for late nights. Never has been.'

'Petunia and Bartram left shortly after Evan told everyone he was having an early night,' Janet informed her, grinning at Evan. 'That was almost two hours ago.'

'Damn it. I should've called and told her what was happening,' Beatrix said. 'Oh well. I'll see her in the morning. So what's been going on since I was last here? I heard about Laurel and Jamie McDay. I can't believe that. Laurel is so lucky. Are they here? Aunty P told me he took her to Hollywood or something but that they'd be coming back here because Jamie is going to be filming in England for a while. Is that true? You know how such things go right over Aunty P's head. I almost had to force even that much out of her. And she had to ask Bartram half of it.'

'You should've called one of us,' Ivy said. 'We'd have told you everything. And yes, they're back. Well... they're not, to be honest. This weekend he's taken her to Rome, but they're back on Wednesday, I think. Her mum'll know. She's running the café while Laurel's away.'

'Wow! Rome,' Lucy said. 'Lucky Laurel.'

Beatrix had told her all about Laurel and Laurel's movie star boyfriend, Jamie McDay. Beatrix was hoping to get to meet him while they were here. Lucy wondered if Beatrix was secretly hoping to be offered a part in the Vampire series in which Jamie starred, but Beatrix hadn't mentioned that and Lucy didn't want to either, in case it got Beatrix's hopes up and nothing came of it. These Hollywood types could be unpredictable, so Lucy had heard, even if they were dating a friend.

'Have you been to Rome, Lucy?' Evan asked.

'No. But it's on my list of places to go.'

'You have to take time off work to go on holiday,'

Beatrix said. 'This week is your first week off in the last two years, I think.'

Lucy shrugged. 'We're busy at work and I'm hoping for a promotion.' The others looked at her as if she were some sort of alien creature – except Evan. He merely nodded as if he understood completely.

'What do you do?' Janet asked.

'I'm a litigation lawyer.'

'Really?' Ivy looked excited. 'Mum might need one of those in the not too distant future. She's having problems with some builders, aren't you, Mum?'

'That's the understatement of the year,' Janet replied.

Lucy shook her head. 'Commercial litigation, I'm afraid. Not civil. Although I'd be happy to help you out, of course, and point you in the right direction. Is it really that bad that you need to resort to litigation?'

'It's either that or murder. Do you know any good criminal lawyers?' Janet wasn't smiling.

'Er. One or two. But I'd advise against it, if possible. I'd also advise against litigation, if at all possible. It's worth pursuing other options, if there are any, before going down that route.'

'A lawyer who's not trying to get you to sue someone,' Evan remarked. 'That's a first.'

'We're not all like some of those ambulance chasers you see on TV. Most of us have… morals.' Was that actually true? She liked to think so but she wasn't one hundred per cent convinced, herself.

'So tell us more about yourself, Lucy,' Janet said. So far we know you're a commercial lawyer with morals. That must be rarer than hen's teeth. Do you have a boyfriend?'

Lucy shook her head. Why had Janet glanced at Evan when she'd asked that? He clearly noticed it and he didn't

30

look best pleased.

'No boyfriend. But there is a guy at work I'm interested in. I don't think anything will come of it though.'

Beatrix smiled. 'What about you, Evan? Do you have a girlfriend?'

'What!' He looked terrified. 'No. And I'm not looking for one either.'

'Oh,' Lucy said. And emptied her glass.

'You weren't kidding about the bottle, were you? Another?' Janet took the glass and waggled it in front of Lucy.

'Yes please. I'm on holiday, after all.'

'And you've got those bats to face on the walk home,' Ivy reminded her, grinning devilishly.

'Don't worry about the bats,' Holly told her. 'My boyfriend, Gabriel will be returning from a meeting in London any time soon. He'll happily give you all a lift back to the cottages when he comes to pick me up. We live in Holly Cottage, so it's not even out of our way.'

'Thank God for that,' Lucy said.

'No,' Ivy corrected. 'You mean, thank the angel, Gabriel.'

31

Chapter Four

Lucy's head was thumping and her eyes felt as if they were swimming in a bowl of boiling water. Exactly how much had she had to drink last night? She hoped she had not consumed the entire bottle as she had joked but she must have downed at least half of it because she could not remember coming home. Where was she anyway and what time was it? She forced her eyes to focus on the apple-green walls. Oh yes. Mistletoe Cottage.

She managed to lift her arm and glance at her watch. Five-fifteen. In the morning! Dear God. How could it be so bright at five-fifteen a.m? Soft yellow rays of early morning sun shot through the chinks in the curtains and pierced her eyes. She closed them and turned over. At least the bed was comfortable. She could stay here all day. It was Saturday after all, and she was on holiday.

No, she could not. Her pounding head demanded attention and her parched throat urgently required refreshment. She needed aspirin and coffee. Right now.

She reluctantly dragged herself out of bed. Where were her things? All she could see were her clothes from last night, strewn across the floor. And why was her bra hanging from the door handle? She shivered as a cool breeze teased her hair and stroked her naked body. Naked? Why was she naked? She always wore cotton shorts and a T-shirt top to bed in the summer. She never slept naked. Ever. Unless she spent the night with a... Oh. My. Dear. God! She hadn't, had she? Her headache momentarily forgotten, her eyes frantically scanned the room.

Oh shit! This wasn't the room she'd been in yesterday evening. She closed her eyes and prayed silently. Please let this be Beatrix's room. Please let us have simply gone to the wrong rooms last night. Please don't let this mean...

A gentle knock on the half-open door made her heart leap to her throat and when a head of thick blond hair came into view, her heart almost left her body.

'No! Oh please God. No.'

She shut her eyes tight in the vain hope that when she reopened them she would find this was merely a dream. A strange and exceedingly vivid dream, but just that. A dream.

She took a deep breath and summoned her courage. But when she opened her eyes, Evan Foster stood before her. He was wearing a pair of shorts and a T-shirt and from the look of his dishevelled hair and ruddy complexion, he must have been out running, or doing something equally energetic. His eyes were closed and his head averted to one side, and he held a mug of coffee in his hands.

'Er. Good morning. I don't know how you take your coffee, so it's just with milk. If you get back into bed, I'll bring it over.'

'What? You want to trade a mug of coffee for sex? Are you bloody mad?'

His eyes shot open but he quickly closed them again and a rash of even darker red crept across his crimson face.

'No! I didn't mean it like that. I meant... if you cover

33

yourself up, I can open my eyes and bring you the coffee. You're… you're naked.'

She glanced down at herself, gasped as she remembered he was right, and yanked at the duvet.

'I think it's a bit bloody late for that,' she said, but she pulled the duvet tightly around her. 'What the hell happened last night and how did I end up in what I assume is your bed? Wait. Before you answer that, do you have any aspirin? Or do you know where my handbag is? I've got some in there. You can open your eyes. I'm decent.'

He seemed to do all he could not to meet her gaze as he brought over the coffee and held it out to her from a distance, as if he were afraid to get too close.

'I think I saw your bag downstairs. I'll get it. Take this.'

'Thanks,' she said, with some reluctance, and took the mug. The second it had left his hand, he turned on his heel and was gone. 'I wonder if you moved that fast last night,' she mumbled under her breath. She shook her head – which was a mistake, and waited for the bolt of pain to subside before she sipped the coffee. Gosh, it was good. The man clearly knew how to handle a coffee machine. She assumed this cottage had one similar to the one in Mistletoe Cottage.

She took three long gulps and sighed. Did he know how to handle a woman? She couldn't remember a thing, so either it was particularly earth-shatteringly memorable, or she was suffering from alcohol induced memory loss. For some reason she hoped it was the latter. She had no idea why but she got the impression that Evan Foster would actually be pretty good in bed.

She quivered as strange sensations danced through her. It was a pity she couldn't remember, especially as last night was her first ever one-night stand. A girl should remember that sort of thing. Or perhaps not.

Evan returned with her bag and again held it out to her from a safe distance.

Lucy almost laughed as she took it. 'I don't have any communicable diseases, you know. And if I did have, don't you think it's a bit late to be keeping your distance? I assume we got pretty close last night.'

Was he blushing? Was the guy actually embarrassed?

'I… Um.'

Now she did laugh.

'I take it from your demeanour this morning that either, one, you seriously regret last night, or two, you don't do this very often and haven't got the faintest clue how to behave or what to say.' She popped two aspirin in her mouth and swallowed them down with a swig of coffee.

'Do you think this is funny?' He looked cross. 'I do regret it. Although I'm not sure anything serious actually happened. I don't think either of us were capable of very much. And no, I don't do this kind of thing on a regular basis. In fact I can safely say, you're the first.'

'What! Seriously? Are you telling me you're a… a virgin?' This was unbelievable.

'Don't be ridiculous. I'm thirty-two years old. Of course I'm not a virgin. What I meant was, I don't sleep around and I definitely don't have one-night stands.'

'Okay. Keep your shirt on.' She took another gulp of coffee. 'Although the evidence before us seems to negate that statement. This is excellent coffee, by the way.'

He blinked and dragged his hand through his hair.

'I assume you do this sort of thing all the time.'

She spat coffee all over the duvet and glowered at him. 'No, Evan. I don't. It may interest you to know that this is a first for me, too. Not sex, of course. A one-night stand. Although why it's called that is beyond me. I don't think there's much standing involved. Unless you're outside a pub or...' She saw the startled expression on his face and coughed lightly. 'Never mind. Um. I think I'd better get dressed and go next door. I don't expect Beatrix will be up yet so I hope she's left the key under the geranium.'

'What? Er. I don't think she's there. I vaguely remember her going off with someone in the pub. I think it was Harry but I could be wrong. I'm sure she left before we did though.'

That was news. 'Seriously? Beatrix left me and went off with some strange guy. Why didn't you stop her?'

'I... It wasn't any of my business. I only met you both last night. I can't tell either of you what to do or who you can go off with. Besides, Harry's not strange – well not that strange. He's my cousin. And I'm pretty sure Beatrix knows him. They seemed very friendly.'

'People usually do when they're going to have sex. And you seem to remember rather a lot about last night. I can't recall any of it. What else happened that you haven't told me? And at what point exactly did your memory – not to mention your morals – conveniently fail you?'

'My morals? Do the words glass houses and stones mean anything to you? You were the one doing all the flirting last night, not me. I seem to recall you couldn't keep your hands off me. I do remember you saying that you'd like to check me over and that it was only fair to return the favour, or something equally banal.'

'Equally banal! Well, I'm sorry to be so unoriginal. Although you could have easily ignored me. It must have been fairly obvious I'd had too much to drink.'

'You're kind of difficult to ignore and you didn't appear to be that drunk. You just seemed a bit tipsy, that's all.'

'So you thought you'd take advantage of my "tipsy"

state?'

'Me take advantage! It may interest to know that you were the one who did that. You were the one who invited yourself in for a nightcap, not me. And you were the one who suggested we keep drinking. We were half way through a bottle of whisky. That's when my memory fails me. And believe me, it wasn't convenient at all. This isn't convenient. This is a sodding nightmare.'

'Well, thank *you* very much! I must have been exceedingly drunk to even consider flirting with such a Neanderthal as you. And as for the whisky, you could have said no at any time. You're a grown man and a pretty strong one from what I can tell. I could hardly have forced you to drink it. And I could hardly have forced myself on you. You must have wanted it as much as I apparently did in my addled state. Now get out. I want to get dressed and go.'

'Thank Christ for that. I'm going for another run. Shut the door behind you when you leave.' He turned to go.

'With pleasure. I would say thanks for a good time, but I don't suppose it was. Not for one minute.'

'I told you,' he said, his knuckles white as he gripped the side of the door. 'Nothing actually happened.'

'How can you possibly say that? I can't remember a thing and you've just admitted that your memory was drowned by whisky.'

'That's why I can say it. Believe me, after that much alcohol I couldn't have done anything even if I'd wanted to. And if I had, I would definitely remember it. And so would you, I'm sure.'

'So you're saying you didn't want to? Aren't you the charmer? And so arrogant, too. If you're really such a fantastic lover, how come you don't have a girlfriend? Don't answer that. I really don't care. And for your information, Mr Sex God... being incredibly drunk doesn't always prevent a man from having an erection. It depends on the man. Just because you hope you couldn't doesn't mean you didn't.'

'I wasn't being arrogant. I was stating a fact. Even women who've suffered date rape can usually remember that something happened.'

Lucy gasped. 'Seriously? You're comparing last night with date rape. Is that how you get your women?' She regretted that as soon as she had said it. Date rape was no joking matter.

'No. Is getting men drunk how you get yours? Sorry! I didn't mean that. And I wasn't being arrogant, I was...' He shook his head and sighed, finally meeting her eyes. 'Let's not fight, Lucy. Let's just try and forget last night and move on. You're clearly not really interested in me and I'm definitely not interested in you. I honestly think that if we'd had sex, one of us would remember something about it. Some little thing and... why are you grinning? Oh, for God's sake, woman. Can't you be serious about anything? That was not a double entendre. I was not referring to my dick!'

Lucy coughed. What was wrong with her? She wasn't usually like this. She must be suffering from alcohol poisoning. It must have affected her personality in some weird way. That was the only explanation for her ludicrous and seemingly outrageous behaviour.

'Sorry,' she said, with a shrug. 'Blame the barrel-loads of alcohol. I'm not usually like this, believe me.'

His piercing blue eyes gave her a quick once-over before he turned and left, saying: 'I do believe you, Lucy. I'll leave you to get dressed.'

'Thank you,' she said, but she wasn't sure he heard. She could tell that he was down the stairs and out the door no sooner had she finished speaking.

Chapter Five

'Well, Beatrix,' Lucy said, when Beatrix phoned her at a little after ten-thirty. 'I know you said I needed time out to "find myself" but so far, honey, I'm not liking what I see. I sincerely hope your night was better than mine. And thank you for leaving me, by the way.'

'My pleasure. Oh. You're being sarcastic, aren't you? Didn't you and Evan have a good night then? We could all see you fancied the pants off one another, so I thought you'd be pleased to have me out of the way.'

'Well then, you're clearly all as blind as those bats you were going on about. We didn't and we don't. Well we did, but he assures me nothing happened. And I must admit I think he's right, now that I've had time to think about it. I would remember having sex, wouldn't I? Even bad sex, or over in an instant sex. In fact, it's been so long since I've had sex that I bloody well hope I do remember the next time I have it.'

'Er. I don't have the vaguest idea what you're prattling on about. Did you sleep with Evan or not?'

'Sleep, yes. Have sex, apparently not.'

'Really? Why not?'

'Too drunk, and not interested.'

one day telling her his cricketing history.

She rolled onto her back and opened her eyes. Why did she feel so restless? Usually when she started thinking about Henry she could drift off into sleep within seconds. Henry and his cricket balls were far more reliable than counting sheep. Well, not his cricket balls, exactly.

She smiled up at the ceiling. She could make out several shapes in the stippled plaster. Not quite the Sistine Chapel and the decorator was certainly no Michelangelo, but the swirls and bumps formed images as she scrutinised the white canvas above her. Actually, was it plaster or was it Artex? Ceiling finishes were not something she knew much about. Or anything at all about, if she were to be honest with herself.

Perhaps that was something she should do. Be honest with herself. And maybe she should begin by asking herself why was she wasting time lying in bed staring at the ceiling? She threw the duvet back, tumbled out of bed and headed for the shower.

Ever since Henry had kissed her in the lift last month, she had somehow, felt ill at ease. She'd started questioning her future and doubting her ability. Beatrix had reminded her how far she had come since they were at Uni together, and how amazing it was that Lucy should be a junior associate at such a top-notch law firm, before her thirtieth birthday.

Lucy knew Beatrix was right. She had come a long way – and from relatively humble beginnings. Most of the other junior associates were born with silver spoons in their mouths and their *daddies* knew everyone who was anyone. And yes, even the guys called their dads, daddy, or Pa, or Pater, or some such la-dee-dah name. No one but Lucy called him plain old Dad.

Not that Lucy would ever call her dad, plain. Or old.

He was the best dad any girl could want. Even if he wasn't actually her biological father. But as she had no idea who or where that person was, Desmond Draycourt was her dad in every way bar scientifically.

She had no idea who or where her biological mum was either. It seemed neither culprits wanted her, so they had left her on a step outside the church of St Mary Magdalen where Francesca Draycourt, the woman she thought of as her real mother, had discovered her one September morning shortly after dawn as she was taking, Portia, her Springer Spaniel for an early morning walk.

Lucy had been wrapped in a colourful shawl with a note pinned to it. The note, in rather dramatic fashion and written in an excessively flowing hand, said: *My name is Luciana. I am one year old and my birthday is on August 31st. Please take good care of me and lavish me with love and kindness because the Universe has put me here and I trust it will lead me to better things in life.*

And the Universe had. Well, Lucy assumed it had. There was little chance that her biological parents could have treated her any better than Francesca and Desmond Draycourt had done. The Draycourts had even been kind and considerate enough to change her name from Luciana to Lucy, and for that alone she would be forever in their debt. Added to everything else they'd done for her, she owed them more than several lifetimes could repay. Not that they made her feel as if she owed them anything. Unable to have children of their own, they constantly told her how she was the one who had brought them more joy and happiness beyond their wildest dreams. Even the adoption had gone smoothly. It was as if it was meant to be, Francesca had often said.

Beatrix was forever telling Lucy that the Universe worked in mysterious ways. Perhaps she was right. It had been a long time since Lucy had thought about the day she was found abandoned. She had convinced herself that the abandonment had not affected her in a negative way, but even she knew that it probably had, in spite of the happy life she was leading because of it.

She had no desire to meet or become acquainted with her biological parents if they were still alive, and she had no reason to assume they would not be. But perhaps she would like to know who they were and why they chose not to keep her. Someone clearly thought she would have a better life without them.

She had once thought that her mother may have been a battered wife who hadn't wanted her child to grow up in that environment, but she doubted it. She had of course thought that she may have been a princess, hidden for her own safety from an evil step-mother. Well, every little girl fantasises about being a secret princess, don't they?

The truth of the matter is that she would probably never know. And that didn't really bother her. Or it hadn't until recently. Was it really since that night that Henry had kissed her that she'd started thinking like this? Did she feel in some way deep down that she wasn't sure who she was? Was she worried that there was a possibility that she might suddenly turn into a serial killer or something? Taking after her 'real' father's side of the family, no doubt. Her 'real' mother was probably a kleptomaniac, or some other type of maniac. Lucy did love shopping after all, although she always paid for everything. Now she was being ridiculous. But maybe that was the root of the problem. Perhaps she was slightly worried that nature, rather than nurture, was shaping her future. And all because the senior partner of the litigation department had kissed her? She clearly was the maniac, and the sooner she stopped thinking about this nonsense, the better.

She hurriedly dried herself, threw on some clothes, brushed her hair and dashed out of Mistletoe Cottage into a wall of summer heat. The air was humid and the sun beat down on her bare shoulders as she scrunched across the gravel parking area in the direction of the footpath. A stifling breeze brought additional waves of heat as well as the scent of freshly mown grass. She could vaguely make out a tractor in the far distance, its engine chugging in a gently soothing fashion.

'Are you heading to the village?'

At first she thought it was Evan's voice, and held her breath, only to realise it wasn't the same tone.

'Hello,' she said, turning to face the handsome man with espresso-coffee-coloured hair.

He grinned at her and tipped his head to one side. 'You don't remember me, do you? I'm Gabriel. Gabriel Hardwick. Holly's boyfriend. I gave you a lift home last night. You were pretty drunk, so I'm not surprised.'

'Thank you!' she said. 'Finally! Someone who realised I was completely out of my tree last night and not just tipsy.'

His dark brows knit together. 'Sorry. Am I missing something?'

She shook her head and laughed. 'No. Sorry. Long – and somewhat dubious – story.'

'I see. I'm headed to the village if you want a lift. It'll save you walking in this heat.'

'You really are an angel, aren't you, Gabriel?'

'If I had a pound for the number of times I'd heard that, I'd be a very rich angel. Follow me. The car's over here.'

'Instead of an exceedingly rich author? Oh, I didn't notice there was another parking area on this side of the cottages.'

'Yes. And I'm not sure that I'd class myself as

46

exceedingly rich. My definition of exceedingly rich may be different to yours. Despite what you may have read in the press, not all authors earn a fortune. I'll admit I do pretty well, but I'm not yet on a par with the likes of J K Rowling.'

'No, I can see that from this gleaming red Jaguar. And last night, I do vaguely remember being driven home in a Range Rover. Sorry. Your finances are none of my business. I don't know what's happening to me at the moment. It's as if I'm becoming a completely different person.' She eased into the passenger seat. 'I could get used to this.'

'Isn't that called schizophrenia? Or possibly, alcohol poisoning. Holly said that you all had a lot to drink last night and I know Holly did. She was singing, and she only does that when she is very, very drunk. Ivy on the other hand – you couldn't stop her singing if you tried.'

'Did I meet her boyfriend, Ned last night, too? I know she said he would be joining us but I can't remember seeing him.'

'Yep. Ned was there. You were asking him how many horses he's shod lately.'

'Oh dear, was I? I must have made a really good first impression on the residents of Hideaway Down.'

'I think we can safely say you did. I assume you don't remember chasing the Gaggle Gang down Market Street either?'

'Who? You're joking, aren't you? I chased a group of thugs down the street? Bloody hell. I'm not sure which amazes me more, the fact that I did it or the fact that this place has a gang of thugs.'

'You did but it doesn't. The Gaggle Gang are a flock of geese. They wander freely around the village, although they're shut in at night in case of foxes. But Meg

Stanbridge, the woman who, sort of owns them, hasn't been well and her friend Sarah Saltcote has been looking after both Meg and the geese. It seems she didn't lock up properly last night. Gramps, Janet, Ned and I had to round them up – and you – and take them home.'

Lucy sucked in a long slow breath.

'Well, this is certainly going to be a holiday to remember. I must thank my best friend, Beatrix for not telling about this little fiasco.'

'Beatrix wasn't there. She'd left with Harry long before then. But I'm sure she'll have heard all about it this morning. Where do you want me to drop you?' Gabriel asked as they turned into Market Street.

'Off Hideaway Cliff, if that isn't too much trouble. I trust the fall will kill me outright.'

Gabriel winked at her. 'Don't worry. Far worse happened to me when I first arrived here, and I've ended up living happily ever after. Things are never as bad as they seem. Trust me.'

'Seriously? You're an author. You make things up for a living.'

'True. But you'll be laughing about this by the end of the week. Honestly, you will. Shall I drop you at The Snowdrop Inn?'

'That's perfect, thanks. I'm meeting Beatrix, Petunia and Bartram there for lunch.'

'And Evan, it seems.' Gabriel nodded towards a group of people heading into the pub. That's Petunia and Bartram with him and Beatrix, just going inside.'

'Oh dear God! Can this holiday get any worse?'

Chapter Six

Lucy took a deep breath and marched into The Snowdrop Inn with her head held high. She had no idea what kind of reception she would receive after what Gabriel had just told her but whatever happened she intended to retain some iota of dignity.

'Hello, Lucy,' Janet said, beaming at her as she reached the bar. 'You're looking very summery this morning. G&T?'

'Er. Thank you. I hope I didn't make myself unwelcome last night. I hear I behaved rather badly.'

Janet met her look. 'Don't give it another thought, dear. You enjoyed yourself, I hope, and that's all that matters. Nothing got broken. No one got hurt. Everyone had fun. That's what going to the local pub is all about.' She winked and handed Lucy her drink. 'This one's on me.'

'Oh no, I couldn't. I should be buying you a drink to apologise.' Lucy pulled out her purse.

'Put that away, young lady, or you will make yourself unwelcome.'

The smile remained but Janet's eyes had a steely look about them, so Lucy did as she was told, and returned the smile.

'Thank you. I'm beginning to see why Beatrix raves about Hideaway Down.'

'It's the best place in the world. Beatrix has nipped to the loo but there's a certain young man over there who looks eager to see you.'

Janet nodded towards one end of the pub and Lucy turned to find Evan staring at her. He averted his gaze when she met his eyes.

'You're here!' The door to the toilets slammed shut behind Beatrix and she beckoned Lucy in the direction she was walking, linking her arm through hers. 'You remember Aunty P, of course, and you know Evan. This is Bartram, Lucy.'

A ruddy-faced, slightly overweight man in his fifties, Lucy guessed, stood up and grabbed her hand, shaking it enthusiastically.

'It's lovely to meet you, Lucy. I've been hearing good things about you. You spent last night with my dear nephew Evan, I'm told.'

'What!' Lucy's fingers tightened around her glass and she glowered at Evan.

'In the pub, he means,' Evan said, hastily. 'Beatrix and I were saying that we all spent the evening in here, having met earlier at the cottages.'

'Yes, yes. It's a small world, isn't it?' Bartram said. 'Evan would normally stay with me, or with Beth, but there was a cancellation at the cottages at the last minute, and we all know how much you young people like your independence. It's all worked out very nicely, hasn't it, Petunia, my love? You were right, as always.' He smiled lovingly at Petunia and planted a kiss on her cheek as he resumed his seat.

Petunia blushed, somewhat surprisingly. Lucy hadn't imagined her to be the type. She always seemed so sure of herself when she came to stay and half the time she gave the impression that she wasn't really of this world. She seemed to float around in an aura of heavenly scents and long, flowing dresses. Lucy originally thought Petunia might be on drugs of some sort, but Beatrix assured her it was simply Petunia's way and that she would never dream of taking any form of mind-altering substance. Lucy wished she could achieve such calm. Particularly at the present moment.

Her heart was thumping in her chest, and the perspiration forming on her forehead wasn't simply due to the midday heat. The Snowdrop Inn had air conditioning – albeit something from the 1990s by the look of it, and from the peculiar rattling sounds the large white boxes were making, it might give up the ghost at any time. But she was on edge. Despite her and Evan having parted on fairly amicable terms, given the circumstances, she could cut the tension between them with a knife. He was clearly doing everything in his power to avoid looking at her but when Bartram patted the cushioned bench seat where Evan was sitting, Evan darted a look of abject terror at Lucy.

'Move over, Evan,' Bartram said, 'and let lovely Lucy sit down, there's my boy.'

Evan didn't really have much choice. He slid as far towards the edge as he could.

Beatrix laughed. 'She's not that fat, Evan. She doesn't need that much room. If you slide over any further you'll be on the floor.'

Lucy gave him a quick smile and perched on the other edge, leaving a massive gap between them. She saw the curious look Petunia was giving her and Evan, and she moved slightly towards him so as not to raise any questions.

'We're so pleased you could take time off work to come and stay, Lucy,' Petunia said. 'I know how busy you are and how important your career is to you. We hope you have a wonderful week here in Hideaway Down. It's a small place, but it has so much to offer if you give it a chance. Janet Gilroy always says that anything can happen in Hideaway Down, and she's right. I mean, look at us.'

She took Bartram's hand in hers and kissed it. 'Who would have thought that we'd fall in love? We seem to have little in common, but love doesn't have a checklist it ticks off. It simply throws two people together, fills their hearts with mutual joy and before they know it, they find they want to share their lives with one another.'

Was Petunia trying to tell her something?

'I'm not looking for love, if that's what you're saying. I'm here because Beatrix asked me to come and because I haven't had a holiday in a very long time. Love is the last thing on my mind.'

Petunia smiled. 'That's when it usually takes us by surprise – when we're not looking for it. But no, I wasn't suggesting you were. Although the Universe works in mysterious ways and sometimes...' She shrugged and raised her glass to her lips, smiling into it without finishing her sentence.

'Let me get some more drinks.' Evan leapt to his feet. 'The same again for everyone?'

'Not for me,' Lucy said. 'I'm going to take it easy today.'

'Very sensible,' Evan replied, giving her a quick glance.

'Love certainly took me by surprise last night,' Beatrix said in a hushed tone, leaning towards Lucy. 'Well, not love exactly, but you know what I mean.' She nodded towards Petunia and Bartram, who were staring into each other's eyes as if they shared some special secret and were conveying it to one another telepathically. 'That's love. Look at them. They're virtually oblivious to us.'

Lucy looked at them for a moment before shifting closer to Beatrix. 'So tell me everything. What's he like? Are you going to be seeing him again? Is he local?'

Beatrix grinned. 'You met him. Don't you remember?'

Lucy shook her head. 'Nope. And from what I've heard from Gabriel, that's probably a good thing.'

'What's Gabriel been saying about Harry?' Beatrix boomed out, attracting more than just Petunia and Bartram's attention.

'What, sweetheart?' Petunia queried. 'I didn't quite catch what you said.'

Beatrix blushed and lowered her voice. 'Sorry. I was discussing something with Lucy. I didn't mean to shout.'

Petunia smiled and Lucy continued: 'Not about Harry. About me and some geese.'

'Oh yes. I heard about that.' Beatrix sounded relieved. 'Do you honestly not remember anything? That's a bit worrying, isn't it?'

'You have no idea,' Lucy said. 'What's even more worrying is that I seem to have metamorphosed into some mad woman. I don't usually behave like this, you know that. I'm careful not to let myself get out of control and show myself up, especially with the people at work. How can I have gone so berserk in just one night?'

'Perhaps you're making up for lost time. Perhaps the countryside and sea air are bringing out the real you.'

'Bloody hell, I hope not. If this is the real me, I don't want to be real. You... you don't really think it is, do you?'

Beatrix laughed. 'Why're you so worried? All you did was get drunk, chase a few geese and spend the night with

53

a complete stranger. To some women I know, that's a quiet night. You take yourself far too seriously Lucy, that's your trouble. You're so concerned about what everyone at that posh law firm thinks about you and so anxious not to put a foot wrong, that you hold back. The only person there who ever gets to see the real you, is Nikki. Perhaps being away from London has allowed you to feel… free. I would stop worrying, if I were you, and simply go with the flow. Enjoy it, even if it is only for one week and then go back to being the straight-laced, serious, lawyer.'

'I'm not straight-laced. Am I?'

Beatrix pulled a face. 'You're not as much fun as you were at Uni.'

'We were young and carefree in those days. We've grown up since then, that's all.'

'Speak for yourself. I'm still young and carefree. You're the one who wants to take on the world and climb every mountain in your path. Me? I let the world do what it wants and as for mountains, I walk around them. And speaking of mountains, are you absolutely sure nothing happened last night between you and that hunk.' She nodded in Evan's direction as he was returning with the drinks. 'Can't you even remember kissing him? You must have kissed at the very least.'

'Can't remember a thing. Which is probably just as well as he's not in the slightest bit interested in me.'

'So he says.'

'What's that supposed to mean?'

'He's been acting very strangely since last night.'

'He's probably terrified I'll try to seduce him again, and that he'll have to fight me off. Last night has done wonders for my ego, I can tell you.'

'Perhaps he's terrified that he might not want to. Fight

you off, I mean. Aunty P tells me that he's convinced he's still in love with his ex-fiancée, who dumped him and ran off with his best friend and business partner. He's adamant that he's not interested in being with anyone else.'

'Wow! Well he definitely wasn't interested in being with me, that's for sure.'

'How do you know? You can't remember a thing that happened last night. Perhaps it was the other way around. Perhaps you weren't interested in him when it came to doing the deed. Perhaps you said no.'

Lucy tipped her head to one side and raised her eyebrows. 'Seriously? You think I would say no to that body? I'm not that straight-laced, Beatrix, I can assure you.'

'What are you two whispering about?'

'Harry!' Beatrix's eyes lit up. 'Lucy! This is Harry.'

'Hello, Lucy. We met last night so I don't know why Beatrix is introducing me.'

Lucy turned to the athletic-looking young man standing over them, and smiled. 'I don't remember anything about last night. Sorry. It's good to meet you, Harry.'

'Harry Goode, good to meet you again,' he said, cheerily.

'Harry,' Evan said, arriving back at the table. 'I've just got drinks. What would you like?'

'Not for me, thanks. I've just popped in to say hello to Beatrix. I can't stop I'm afraid. There was a bit of a crisis at the milking shed this morning when I was with... elsewhere. I've got to get over there and sort it out. Dad managed a temporary fix but as he told me, this new-fangled machinery is all Chinese to him.' He kissed Beatrix on the cheek, gave everyone a wave and dashed towards the door, saying: 'Have a Goode good day everyone.'

55

'Bye Harry,' Beatrix called after him, looking somewhat stunned.

'Dear Harry,' Bartram said, smiling at Beatrix and then at Lucy. 'He works at Hideaway Farm with his dad, Henry and my sister, Beth. Harry delivers fresh milk to the entire village, including the cottages you're staying in. He's a lovely boy.'

'He's a lovely young man,' Petunia corrected. 'And I believe he's rather keen on my niece.' She grinned knowingly at Beatrix.

'Is he?' Bartram puffed out his florid cheeks. 'Since when?'

'Since yesterday,' Evan said, sitting down again.

'Yesterday?' Bartram's questioning eyes scanned the group's faces. 'What happened yesterday?'

'I'm not sure you'd want to know,' Beatrix said, grinning.

Lucy watched Harry and his wild, bush-like ginger hair disappear; the bell above the doorway tinkled like giggling children as the heavy oak door closed behind him. He looked younger than Lucy had expected but perhaps he was merely lucky enough to have a youthful complexion. He had at least one thing in his favour: he worked for a living, unlike most of Beatrix's previous boyfriends. And he seemed genuinely pleasant – and cheerful. Again, so unlike several of his predecessors. But she mustn't get her hopes up for Beatrix. It was early days after all and they lived at least sixty miles apart. That was hardly conducive to a good, long-term relationship.

'I heard all about young Lucy here,' Bartram said, 'but no one mentioned you or Harry. Not as far as I recall. Did they, sweetheart?' He turned to Petunia.

'No, darling. Let's not worry about it. I'll explain later. For now, let's discuss our wedding. I've got something to

56

ask Lucy and haven't you got something you want to ask Evan?'

Lucy didn't like the sound of that. Warning bells jangled in her ears – or perhaps someone had opened the pub door – but there was definitely a tone in Petunia's voice. And a rather disconcerting one at that.

'O... kay.' Lucy held her breath.

Petunia smiled. 'Don't look so worried, dear. I just want to ask if you'd be a bridesmaid at our wedding. Beatrix is maid of honour, and she'll be followed by Holly and Ivy, and then Laurel. I think it would be lovely to have another bridesmaid next to Laurel. Please say you will.'

'Um. I'd be delighted, of course,' Lucy lied, sending Beatrix a pleading look. The last thing she wanted to be was a bridesmaid. She'd undoubtedly do something stupid and mess up the whole day. 'But the wedding's next weekend. Surely there isn't enough time to sort out an extra dress. Please don't think you have to ask me because you're concerned I feel left out or something. I don't. Honestly. And I'm a bit of a liability at such occasions.'

'I'm sure you're not,' Petunia insisted, smiling reassuringly. 'And... well the truth is, we've already got your dress. Beatrix wants you to be a part of our wedding as much as my darling husband to be and I do. Please, Lucy. It would be such a wonderful gift to us.'

Bloody hell, this woman was good. But Beatrix would pay for this later, Lucy would make sure of that.

'Well then, it seems I can't really say no. Um. Thank you, Petunia. It'd be an honour. I hope you don't live to regret it.'

'Listen,' Beatrix said, laughing. 'The Gaggle Gang will be taking pride of place in front of me. If anyone is going to screw up this wedding, it's them, so you've got nothing to worry about. Which reminds me, what did Kev the Rev say about the geese, Aunty P?'

Petunia and Bartram exchanged amused looks. 'He said that they would probably be better behaved than some of the guests. You know our dear Reverend. He's game for anything. Audrey Stelling, poor love, was a little taken aback at the thought of geese waddling around the church and she's told us that they had better not eat the flowers, but she's fine with the idea now. I think Ned had a word with her. Oh, Ned's Audrey's son, Lucy. She's a darling but she takes such pride in keeping the church looking pristine, so I can hardly blame her.'

'What did you want to ask me?' Evan said, looking mildly perturbed. 'I don't look good in lilac so please don't ask me to be a bridesmaid too.'

Bartram guffawed and slapped Evan's knee. 'No, no, my boy. Not a bridesmaid.' He grew suddenly serious. 'I'd like you to be my best man. It would make me feel as if a part of our darling Chrissie was standing beside me.'

Evan was clearly stunned. He blinked several times, darted a look at Lucy for some reason, and took a large gulp of his beer.

'I don't know what to say,' he finally replied. 'I'll be proud to stand beside you, Uncle. Thank you.'

'Great,' Beatrix said. 'Now that everything's settled, can we order lunch? I'm starving.'

Chapter Seven

'Lordy, lordy me. Has the August Fair arrived already?'

Lucy glanced at the elderly woman with a mass of grey, dishevelled curls and a cherubic face the colour of strawberries, who had come to stand beside her as she stopped to look in the window of The Book Orchard.

'Sorry. Were you speaking to me? I'm not a local so I can't help you with that, I'm afraid.'

'I know you're not a local, dear, of course I do. That's why I asked. Lordy, lordy me, as if I don't know everyone who lives hereabouts. Aren't you with the August Fair? Aren't you one of them Romanies? You look like one, you do.'

Should she be offended? The woman was clearly not all there. Perhaps she meant it as a compliment.

'I'm Lucy Draycourt, Beatrix Welsley's friend. Do you know Beatrix?'

'Know Beatrix? I've known Beatrix nearly all her life, I have. Lucy Draycourt, you say? Hmm. Oh Lordy, lordy, me. You're the posh lawyer Beatrix lives with, you are. Well I never. Here for the wedding, are you? I remember Petunia saying you're one of the bridesmaids, I do. Well it's lovely to meet you, Lucy, it is. I'm Meg. Meg

Stanbridge.'

'The owner of the geese?' Lucy swallowed, and wished she hadn't said that out loud.

'Lordy, lordy, yes. I hear you helped to catch them last night, you did. When that old fool, my friend, Sarah Saltcote let them out, she did. I haven't been well, you know. Better today. Just on my way to The Snowdrop Inn for a medicinal rum, I am. Where's young Beatrix? I'd like to say hello, I would.'

'Oh. Um. She's with Petunia. They're putting the finishing touches to the bridesmaid dresses.'

'Lordy, lordy, you're not helping?'

'No. I'm more of a hindrance when it comes to making things. I did offer but they both suggested I take a look around the village instead.'

Meg chuckled. 'Wanted you out of the way, they did.'

'Evidently. Well, it was good to meet you, Meg. I'm going to pop in here and buy some books.'

'It's dear, Holly Gilroy's bookshop, it is. Have you met the Gilroys? Staying in the cottages, aren't you? So happy she's finally found love. Dumped by her boyfriend, she was. Then along comes Gabriel and bam.' She clapped her hands together, making Lucy jump. 'Love does that, it does. Comes along when we least expect it and knocks us for six, it does. And he's an author, he is.'

'Yes. Enjoy your drink. Glad you're feeling better. Bye for now.' Lucy dashed into The Book Orchard and closed the door firmly behind her.

'I see you've met Meg.' Holly climbed down from the book ladder, from which she'd been stacking the top shelves, and grinned. 'She's rather special. If you want to know who's doing what with whom, Meg will probably be able to tell you.'

'She thought I was a gypsy – well a Romany to be

60

precise. She asked if the August Fair was here.' Lucy shook her head and laughed. 'I suppose it's because of my hair.'

Holly nodded. 'You do have a touch of the Romany about you, especially with the off-the-shoulder dress you're wearing.'

Ivy appeared from behind a door, a mug in each hand and a broad smile plastered across her face. 'And you were a bit of a wild child last night from what I hear. How did things go with the gorgeous Evan? Was he as good as I imagine him to be?'

'Ivy!' Holly snapped. 'I told you that in confidence.'

Ivy raised her brows. 'Oh yeah. I forgot.' She shrugged her shoulders and grinned. 'Well, was he?'

It took Lucy a moment to regain her composure. What was the point in being coy? She may as well just come right out with it.

'I was too drunk to remember and apparently, he was too drunk to show me.'

'Really?' Ivy was clearly surprised. 'You didn't look that... oh. You've obviously heard that several times already, from the expression on your face. Oh well. There's always tonight. Just don't drink so much.'

'Tonight? You must be joking. Nothing's going to happen between me and Evan tonight or any other night. He made that abundantly clear.'

'Did he? Bloody cheek.' Ivy seemed annoyed.

'Yes. Anyway, I'm going to have an early night and the only thing I have any interest in taking to bed with me is a good book – which is why I'm here. Can you recommend something, Holly?'

'I can thoroughly recommend Gabriella Mann's books. Both the early ones, written by Gabriella herself, or the later ones written by Gabriel under his grandmother's name.' Holly grinned. 'I suppose you've heard the story.'

'Yes. Beatrix told me about it. No disrespect to Gabriel – or his grandmother – but I think I'd like to steer clear of romance novels at the moment. Perhaps a good murder?'

'I don't think there's one called *How to Murder the Man Next Door*,' Ivy joked. 'Perhaps you should try one of those self-help books. *How to Get Your Guy into Bed*, or something like that.'

'Ivy! That's enough. Leave Lucy alone.'

'You know I'm only teasing, don't you, Lucy?'

Lucy nodded. She just wished they'd drop the subject.

'But don't forget,' Holly continued, 'Evan hasn't got over his ex. He thinks he's still in love with her.'

'And you would know all about being in love with your ex,' Ivy said, grinning. She glanced at Lucy. 'My sister was besotted with hers, and thought she'd never get over him – until the day a certain author arrived at the door. Within just a matter of a few days, she'd almost forgotten who Paul Best was, let alone the fact that she'd been crazy about him. Or she thought she had.'

'Thank you!' Holly said. 'But Ivy's right. That's exactly what happened. So you never know.'

'Er. I'm not interested in Evan. There's a guy at work I like. A lot. Whatever happened – or didn't happen – last night was just a drunken aberration. It won't happen again, I assure you.'

'Are you trying to convince us?' Ivy asked. 'Or yourself?'

Lucy forced a smile. 'I'm not trying to convince anyone. I'm simply stating the facts as I know them.'

Ivy grinned at Holly. 'I think that's lawyer-speak for "I'm lying through my teeth but I hope you'll be foolish enough to believe me", isn't it?'

Holly glared at her. 'Ivy! If Lucy says she's not

interested, that's her business, not ours.'

'I wasn't being... snotty or anything,' Lucy said. 'He's handsome, and he's got eyes to die for, but that's it. I'm vaguely attracted to him, as any woman would be, with a body like his. And his voice is quite sexy, I suppose, and he has very soft hands, oddly enough but... What? Why are you giving me that look?'

'Because, Lucy,' Ivy said, for someone who's not interested in Evan Foster, you seem to be listing several rather appealing qualities about the man. And even if neither of you are up for a long-term relationship, would holiday sex be such a bad thing?'

Chapter Eight

Lucy was having the strangest dream. She was dancing bare-footed around a camp fire, waving a tambourine in the air, surrounded by Romanies and their caravans. They were singing and chanting and the air was heavy with the scent of lavender and spiced wine.

'Wake up, Lucy!' Beatrix yelled, shoving the bedroom door open and yanking the duvet off her. 'It's ten o'clock and you've slept long enough. We're all going on a picnic up to Hideaway Hole. Grab your bikini and don't forget the suntan lotion. It's a scorcher.'

'Wh-what?' Lucy sat up and rubbed her sleep filled eyes. 'Ten o'clock? How did I sleep so late? But more to the point, how come you're up so early on a Sunday morning? You never surface until almost noon at home.'

'It's this place.' Beatrix dived onto the bed.

'Beatrix. I nearly poked my eye out!'

Beatrix grinned. 'Sorry. But I love it here. It fills me with life and energy. Not to mention I spent the night with Harry, and he's an early riser. I had no idea that the dawn could be so... breathtakingly beautiful.' She rolled onto her back and spread her arms wide. 'Isn't life incredible? Just when we think it's going nowhere, it gives us a wonderful surprise.'

'I'm so happy for you, Beatrix. But I'd be even happier if you would get off my legs. My feet are going numb.'

Beatrix leapt to her feet, with a broad smile on her face. 'Come on, Lucy. Get up. It's going to be a fabulous day.'

Lucy wasn't convinced, but she scrambled out of bed and headed for the shower.

'There's no time for a shower. Besides we're going swimming, so you don't need one. Hurry up and get dressed. We're meeting outside the church in half an hour.'

'I am not leaving this cottage until I've had a shower. Tell me how to get to this place and I'll meet you there.'

'The church or Hideaway Hole?'

'The Hole. I have to say though, it doesn't sound very appealing.'

'You wait until you see it. It's stunningly gorgeous. It's a small, natural lake that's fed by one of the rivers hereabouts, and it's nestled between four hills, one of which is Hideaway Hill, leading up here, to Hideaway Cliff. There's a little waterfall on the seaside section of Hideaway Cliff called The Old Woman's Tap. In weather like this, it just drips but in the winter it flows, like a tap. It's one of the wonders of this place.'

'Hmm. Okay, it does sound rather nice, but that description didn't tell me how to get there.'

'Oh. From here you just follow the signs on the footpath. The ones leading to Hideaway Hole. Not the ones leading to the village, obviously.'

'I think I can manage that.' Lucy tried again to get to the shower. This time Beatrix didn't stop her and she called over her shoulder, as Beatrix ran downstairs: 'Do I need to bring anything else, Beatrix?'

'Yes. There's a picnic basket for you in the kitchen.

I've packed one for each of us. See you later. Don't get lost.'

Lucy couldn't believe it. Hideaway Down really was having an effect on Beatrix.

It was also having an effect on her. Lucy never slept in. Ever. And she had never slept for as long as she had last night. Beatrix had tried to persuade her to go to the pub, but Lucy stood her ground and insisted that she wanted an early night. Beatrix finally gave in and left her to it. Lucy read the murder mystery she had bought from The Book Orchard until about ten before going to bed. She couldn't even remember falling asleep, which was rather worrying, and to sleep so late was astonishing.

She showered, slipped on an orange and white polka dot sundress over her bikini and put on her flip-flops. She grabbed a sun hat and sun cream, and went into the kitchen to collect the picnic basket. It was just a little after ten-thirty when she closed the door of Mistletoe Cottage and stepped out into blinding sunshine.

'Damn it.'

'Something wrong?'

She recognised Evan's voice immediately. Using her free hand, she tried to shield her eyes from the sun but it was too bright.

'No. I've simply forgotten my sunglasses.'

'I don't think you have. Unless that's a new style of hairband, I think you'll find they're on your head.'

She reached up. He was right, although she couldn't remember putting them there. Was she losing her mind? This was beginning to get worrying. She slipped them on and smiled.

'I don't know what's the matter with me. I haven't been myself since the minute I arrived here.'

'That sometimes happens when we're out of what we

consider to be our normal environment. I'm sure it's nothing to worry about.'

'But I've got an excellent memory. Or I did have until yesterday. And I always know where things are. I'm almost obsessively organised. Even Nikki, my PA, asks me where to find things.'

'You're on holiday. Perhaps subconsciously, you've switched off. Perhaps you've relaxed your usual stringent way of doing things. I wouldn't worry about it. You'll find that you'll soon slip into your normal routine once you get back to work.'

'You think so?'

'I do. I see you're going to the picnic.'

'Yes. Beatrix made this basket. Well, not the basket, obviously. The picnic inside it.'

'I knew what you meant.'

'Oh. I'd better go. Enjoy your day.'

'I'm going too. To the picnic, I mean. I suppose we may as well walk together.'

Lucy was tempted to tell him to get lost, but she didn't and they fell into step beside one another, walking in silence for a few minutes.

'You don't have a basket,' she eventually said, for want of anything better to say.

'It's at Beth's. Beth Goode, my aunt. I stayed there last night. But I came back here to get my swimming stuff and my sunglasses, so she and my uncle Henry are taking the basket for me.'

'I see. What? Were you worried I might try to seduce you again?'

Lucy bit her lip as heat rushed to her cheeks. Why on earth had she said that? Thank goodness she couldn't see his eyes hidden behind his sunglasses.

'No. I wanted some pointers for my best man speech,

and who knows Bartram better than his sister? I stayed for dinner and we got talking about my mum. She died when I was two, so I didn't get to know her, and even now, it's painful for my dad to talk about her. I value the time I spend with my aunt Beth, and with my uncle Bartram, of course. I love hearing stories of the past and about the things my mum did, and last night, Beth was in a very talkative mood. I think this wedding has reminded both her and Bartram of my mum, more than ever. She was a very special woman. I wish we'd been able to spend more time together.'

Lucy had expected some sarcastic reply. She hadn't expected such complete and open honesty.

'I'm sorry.'

Evan shrugged. 'Here, let me carry that basket. Sorry. I wasn't thinking.'

As he reached out and grabbed the handle, their fingers brushed momentarily. They exchanged glances but Lucy quickly looked away.

'I never knew my real mother,' she said. 'My biological mother, I mean. She abandoned me. Left me wrapped in a shawl with a note pinned to it, outside a church. I'm adopted. I was lucky.'

Oh dear Lord. Why had she told him that?

'I'm sorry. Does it bother you? Did you have a happy childhood? Do you want to talk about it?'

'I had a very happy childhood. As I said, I was lucky. I couldn't have asked for better parents. Does it bother me? I didn't think it did. I'm still not sure if it does, to be honest, but just recently I've been... I don't know. Restless. Wondering if I'm on the right path. I'm a lawyer. I think I told you that. Don't get me wrong, I love the law. I love my job. But I... Well... Sometimes I feel as if I'm climbing a mountain covered in snow and ice and I can't wait to reach the top because I think it'll be warm and cosy up there. And I'm scared to look down, not just in case I fall, but in case I might decide I'll be even more warm and cosy in the valley below me. Does that make any sense? Any sense at all?'

'It makes perfect sense, Lucy. You obviously want to be at the peak of your profession and you probably have to sacrifice quite a lot in order to get there. Perhaps you're simply wondering if it'll all be worth it. Sometimes we really think we want something, but then we get it, and we find out it's not what we want, after all. Have you met Gordon Gilroy? Everyone calls him Gramps. He's Janet's dad.'

Lucy shook her head. 'No. Does he live here?'

'Yes. He'll probably be at the picnic today. Anyway, he's always full of advice. Every time I come here, he gives me some. Sometimes it's good, sometimes it's not. I haven't seen him for ages because I haven't been here for a long time but I bumped into him last night, on my way to Beth's. I think I told you that I'm still in love with Diana, my ex-fiancée and that I'd take her back in a heartbeat. Gramps knows that.' Evan laughed half-heartedly. 'Everyone knows that. Last night he said: 'Timing is everything, lad. Life gives us what we need, not necessarily what we ask for or what we think we want.' I'm not entirely sure what he meant regarding my situation, but perhaps that's what's happening to you. Perhaps life is going to give you what you need, and it may not be what you think you want.'

'Hmm.' Lucy thought about that for a moment. 'Maybe. And perhaps life is going to do the same to you. You think you want Diana, but maybe life thinks you don't need her.'

Their eyes met and this time Lucy didn't look away.

69

Evan stopped walking and so did she.

'Maybe,' Evan said. 'Although—'

'Lucy! Evan! Coo-ey!' Beatrix called out in the distance, waving like a maniac as if she thought they might not be able to see her.

Lucy sighed. As usual, Beatrix's timing was incredibly bad.

Chapter Nine

Lucy marvelled at the sight before her. The banks surrounding Hideaway Hole were steep on the side where Hideaway Hill led on to Hideaway Cliff, but on the two sides running in parallel away from Hideaway Hill, they gently sloped down to a flat, almost shelf-like plain which joined the parallels. From this large flat area of grassy rock, a small flight of steps had been carved, leading down to the clear blue waters of Hideaway Hole. It looked as if it were possible for visitors to walk into the water if they chose. Several youngsters preferred to jump straight in, it seemed, rather than use the steps, and the area of grassy rock also served as a makeshift beach on which towels were spread, and sun chairs unfolded.

'I think I'm beginning to see why Beatrix says that Hideaway Down has so much to offer,' Lucy said. 'Although why people come here when there are miles of beach on the other side of the cliff is odd.'

'Not really,' Evan replied. 'In weather like this, the beach will be packed on a Sunday, whereas only the locals and others who have visited, know this place exists. And of course, because you have to walk to get here rather than drive, even some who do know about it, prefer to take their cars and park as close to the beach as possible.'

'The water looks bitterly cold.'

'It is. But once you're in, you soon get used to it.'

'I think I may just sunbathe.'

'Coward.'

'I think you meant sensible.'

Evan laughed. 'No. I meant coward.'

'I'd rather be a coward than freeze to death.'

'I'll warm you up. I mean… you'll soon warm up... if you wrap yourself in your towel. Or simply from the heat of the sun.'

'Damn! I just realised I forgot to bring a towel.'

'Beth will have some. She's bringing one for me, and she's bound to bring extra. She always does. Extra towels. Extra cups. Extra plates. Extra food. You name it, Beth will have brought extra.'

Lucy liked the sound of Evan's laugh as he told her that. He'd clearly been embarrassed by his offer to warm her up and had been at pains to backtrack, but when he spoke about his family, all traces of tension or anxiety simply drained away. She found herself wondering why his ex-fiancée Diana had left him for someone else. He seemed so… genuinely honest. And just plain nice. Providing of course you forgot, or at least forgave, his comments of yesterday morning after they had spent the night together.

'How long were you and Diana together?'

Evan glowered at her. 'What?'

'I said—'

'I heard what you said. Why do you want to know?'

'There's no need to bite my head off. I'm sorry I asked. I was merely curious. Forget I mentioned it.'

She marched on ahead but he caught up with her.

'Sorry,' he said. 'I was just surprised, that's all. It's no

72

big secret. We'd been together since college, so about ten and a half years before... we got engaged. She left me about six months after I proposed, give or take a few days. She ran off with my best friend and business partner, Darren. I have no idea how long they'd been seeing one another, but I think perhaps it had started before our engagement. That was one of the reasons I proposed. Oh, not because I thought she was seeing someone else, but because I thought she was getting tired of waiting for me to ask. I clearly misread the signals. She wasn't getting tired of waiting for me to propose. She was getting tired of *me*.'

'Then why did she say yes?'

Evan shrugged. 'That's something you'd have to ask her. She never told me. We'd been together for so long that perhaps she hoped we could get over the rough patch she obviously felt we were going through. I just thought we were starting to drift apart because I was spending so much time developing the business. She often complained that all I did was work. All I cared about was growing the business – and I suppose that was true to a certain extent. But I honestly thought it was what we both wanted. I thought I was doing it for us. Clearly, I should have taken a moment to stop and ask her what she wanted, but I didn't. When she decided she didn't want me or the business, I can truthfully say that it came as a complete shock. What does that tell you about me?'

'It tells me that you work hard and aim high. You can't take all the blame you know. There were two of you in the relationship. Instead of simply complaining, she could have sat you down and made you discuss it. She could have told you exactly how she felt and what she wanted. And to be honest, Evan, I think it was totally selfish of her to continue her relationship with you while she also carried on an affair behind your back with your friend and business partner. Extremely selfish of them both, in fact. Friends and lovers don't behave like that. Or at least they shouldn't.'

He didn't respond but there was something in his eyes that told her she had given him something to think about.

'C'mon you two,' Beatrix yelled, as they reached the flat plain. 'Don't take all day. You can continue your little tête-à-tête after we've had a swim.'

'There's no point in waiting for me, Bea. I'm not going in there for anything.'

'The old Lucy would've. The one before she got all serious and career-driven. The one who thought life was for living and for having fun.'

It was a challenge if ever Lucy had heard one.

'You mean the Lucy who didn't have a mortgage to pay or clients to keep happy or a boss to impress?'

'You're on holiday,' Beatrix said, grinning. 'Evan's going in, aren't you, Evan?'

'Yes.'

Lucy remembered his offer to warm her up. What the hell? Beatrix was right. The old Lucy would have done it. She tossed her sunhat onto the picnic blanket on which Beatrix was standing, kicked off her flip-flops, slipped her sundress over her head and ran to the water's edge. She hesitated for a fraction of a second and Evan shot past her, bringing his knees up to his chest as he leapt into the water. She caught a glimpse of his tanned, toned body and leapt in after him, rising to the surface just inches from his face, her teeth chattering and her entire body shivering from the cold.

'Oh… my… God!... It's… bloody… freezing!'

'Swim,' Evan said, his voice only slightly shaking. 'You'll soon forget the cold.'

'I… can't feel my… toes. Or my… legs.'

Evan reached out and pulled her to him, rubbing his hands over her arms and shoulders.

'Better?'

She was shivering even more, but mainly because her mind had begun to fill with images of him without his swim shorts. And of his body pressed against hers.

Beatrix suddenly jumped in beside her and the image was gone as a plume of water cascaded over her head, sending a shockwave of cold tearing through her body once again.

Chapter Ten

'I look like a beetroot!' Lucy peered at her reflection in the full-length mirror hanging in the hallway of Mistletoe Cottage. 'That sun cream clearly doesn't work very well. I'm burning up.'

'Go and have a hot bath. Then I'll smother you in after-sun. Are you coming to the pub tonight?'

'You must be joking. Look at me, Beatrix. Even my head feels burnt. There's no way I'm going to be able to put clothes on tonight.'

'You can always go in your bikini. I'm sure Evan will appreciate that. I don't think he could keep his eyes off you today, not to mention his hands. I saw him giving you a rub-down under the water. For someone who says he's not interested in you, he's doing a pretty good job of making everyone think he is.'

Lucy frowned. 'I know. I don't get it. But I think there's a very strong possibility that he may just consider me a new friend. Nothing more.'

'You like him, don't you? I mean... really like him.'

'Do I? I can't decide. One minute I think I do, and the next, he's irritating me. I mean, what's all this nonsense about him still being in love with his ex? It's been two years since she left. Does he honestly believe she's going to come back? And why would you want someone who betrayed your trust in such a way? I certainly wouldn't take someone back if they'd cheated on me. Would you?'

Beatrix considered the matter, chewing her bottom lip and twirling her hair between her fingers.

'No. I don't think I would. But perhaps if it came to it, Evan wouldn't either. Perhaps he just tells himself that as a sort of a safety net. You know. So that he doesn't have to get involved with anyone else and risk getting hurt again. He was with her for a long time. I'm not even sure he's had any other girlfriends. He might be scared. Terrified even, of starting again and finding it all falls apart. Break-ups like that can really affect people very badly. It may be the break-up he's still trying to get over, not the actual woman.'

'I hadn't considered that. It's actually very astute of you.'

'So does that mean you'll come to the pub?'

'No, Beatrix, it doesn't. It means I'm going to follow your first suggestion of the bath and the lotion. But don't let me stop you from going. I'll carry on reading my book and have another early night. This place is so relaxing, and I'm actually enjoying it.'

'You? Enjoying relaxing? I never thought I'd hear you say those words.'

Lucy smiled and gingerly made her way upstairs. Even the backs of her legs hurt. She eased herself into a tepid bath which felt like scolding acid the moment she stepped into it.

'Ouch! Ouch! Ouch!'

'Are you okay up there?' Beatrix called up the stairs.

'Does it sound like I'm okay? I'm in agony. I think I'll probably die.'

'Okay then. In that case you don't need me.'

Lucy finally settled back into the water and closed her eyes.

Was that the front door? Something had banged shut. Had Beatrix gone out? Had she meant that Lucy wouldn't need her? Had she gone to the pub? She was going to cover Lucy's body in after-sun. She promised she would.

Another bang. That was definitely the front door. What a relief. Beatrix had obviously just popped out, possibly to the car, and come back. Thank goodness for that. And now she was coming up the stairs.

'Hello? Lucy? Beatrix told me to come up. She said you wanted my help with something. Lucy, where are you?'

That was Evan's voice. Bloody Beatrix! What did she think she was doing?

'I'm in the bath! Don't come in. I don't need you. Beatrix was joking.'

His footsteps stopped outside the half-open bathroom door and Lucy held her breath.

'Oh,' he said, a hint of disappointment in his tone. 'Um. Are you coming to the pub?'

'No. You saw how sunburnt I got. The thought of putting clothes on, let alone sitting in a pub, surrounded by people who might brush against my skin, isn't a cheerful prospect. I'm going to stay in and read. Has Beatrix gone?'

'Yes.'

'Damn it.'

'Anything I can do?'

'No. No thank you.'

'You shouldn't stay in that bath too long. It's great to counteract the sting of the heat, but longer than a few minutes and your skin will start to dry out. You need to smother yourself in after-sun, or some other lotion.'

'Yes. That's what Beatrix said she'd do.'

'I can do it.'

'Thanks. But no.'

'Why not? You can put your bikini back on if you're worried about me seeing you naked. Although you were naked in my bed on Friday night, so technically, that ship has sailed. Or I could close my eyes.'

'Stop laughing. It's not funny. I'm in pain.'

'Then let me help you.'

She wasn't sure which was worse. The thought of Evan seeing her naked and sunburnt. Or the thought of her being naked and so sunburnt that even with Evan smoothing lotion all over her, she would be in too much pain to enjoy it.

'Okay,' she said, having given the matter serious consideration. 'Go downstairs please and come back up in ten minutes. I'm going to hold a towel around me and get on my bed. As you don't find me attractive, it shouldn't be a problem.'

He didn't answer, but the creaking stairs assured her he was on his way down. She hoped he wouldn't walk out the door as Beatrix had.

Chapter Eleven

Lucy was getting the distinct impression that Evan was avoiding her.

She had not seen him since Sunday night when he had gently massaged soothing after-sun onto her tender, sunburnt body. Even at the time, she was sure he was beginning to regret his offer, and to wish that he had gone to the pub instead; he had hardly said a word from the second he entered her bedroom until the moment he left, some thirty minutes later.

But he wasn't the only one who had found it difficult to speak. With each touch, the combination of the cool lotion and the warmth of his hands sent a mixture of searing pain and almost unbearable excitement coursing through her. She had to prevent herself from begging him not to stop. She had somehow managed to control herself, merely thanking him in a friendly manner when he told her he had finished and that it was time he left.

On Monday afternoon she ventured out, having spent twenty minutes deciding what to wear. Still unable to tolerate material against her skin, she chose the skimpiest dress she had brought with her. She had not meant to, but she found herself looking for Evan.

He wasn't in The Coffee Hideaway when she and Beatrix popped in for a cup of tea, Lucy perching painfully on the edge of the seat. Nor was he in The Book Orchard when she called in to buy another book. And he wasn't in The Snowdrop Inn either, where she accompanied Beatrix and Harry for an ice-cold glass of white wine, shortly after seven p.m. They stayed until ten-thirty but there was no sign of Evan when they left, and there were no lights on in Ivy Cottage when Harry walked Lucy and Beatrix home.

Once or twice during the afternoon she had asked if anyone had seen him. Trixie French had served him a large cappuccino in the morning. Holly had seen him chatting to Kev the Rev around eleven, and he had eaten lunch in The Snowdrop Inn with his uncle Henry, shortly after twelve, so Gramps had informed her. Janet had overheard Evan say that he and Beth were going into Eastbourne with Bartram for the final fitting of Bartram's wedding suit, but Lucy's subsequent enquiries all drew a blank. Perhaps she would see him on Tuesday.

But Tuesday came and went, and Lucy still had not seen Evan. Her sunburnt skin was far less red, more a shade of brown and the pain had eased considerably.

In the morning she went with Beatrix to Petunia's for a fitting of their dresses, and afterwards she spent a small fortune on scented soaps, and soothing bath oils in Petunia's Perfumery. That led to a long, leisurely lunch at The Snowdrop Inn where she saw everyone and their dogs, but there was still no sign of Evan.

In the afternoon she popped into the church hall for a meeting of The Hideaway Cliff Preservation Trust, in the vain hope that he might be there. He had mentioned in passing on Sunday that the cliff was now eroding at an alarming rate and that Jarvis Pope was the man to get something done about it. Evan was not there, but Lucy did learn a little about sea damage prevention.

She fell asleep in the armchair in the evening and was woken by the scrunch of wheels on gravel, but by the time she reached the window and peered out into the twilight, Evan's car was empty and the door of Ivy Cottage firmly shut behind him. She considered popping round, merely to say hello, but it sounded so foolish even to her that she went back to her chair and wished that Wednesday would hurry up and come.

By the time it did, Lucy had almost given up hope of seeing him. Hideaway Down was such a small place and yet it seemed it was easier to avoid someone here, if you wanted to, than it was in London.

'Laurel's back today,' Beatrix said, bringing Lucy a steaming mug of delicious-smelling coffee at seven-thirty in the morning.

Lucy still could not get used to this. Beatrix never got up before nine on weekdays at home, long after Lucy left for work... so it could have been later for all she knew. Yet since they had been here their roles seemed to have reversed: Beatrix got up early; Lucy got up late.

Lucy struggled to sit up.

'And that makes you so happy because...'

She took the mug from Beatrix and cradled it in her hands, stretching the muscles in her face back and forth and up and down in an attempt to fully wake up.

'Because that means Jamie McDay will be in town. Well, by town, I mean village of course.'

She plonked herself on the bed, making Lucy spill her coffee.

'Beatrix!'

Lucy grabbed a handful of tissues from the box beside her bed and mopped up the pool of liquid.

'Sorry,' Beatrix said. 'But it's Jamie McDay, Lucy. Jamie McDay.'

'I heard you the first time. I agree that's pretty exciting but it's only seven-thirty. Please don't tell me you're thinking of calling round to see them at this time in the morning.'

'Don't be silly. We're going for breakfast at The Coffee Hideaway. Get up.'

'Er. Does that mean you and me? Do I have to? Can't you go with Harry?'

'Nah. He's got his milk round to do. What is wrong with you? You're always up early in London.'

'It's the sea air. Or the country air. Or maybe the lack of air. It's stifling already.'

'I know. The forecast says it's going to reach thirty-five degrees today. I think it's a day to spend at Hideaway Hole, don't you? After I've had a chat with Jamie McDay, of course.'

'Of course. But I'm not going anywhere near that Hell Hole without at least factor fifty suntan lotion.'

'Come on then. Shake a leg. I told Evan we'd meet him outside at eight.'

Beatrix leapt off the bed, spilling Lucy's coffee once again.

'Oh bloody hell, Beatrix!'

Wait a minute. Had Beatrix just said they were meeting Evan at eight?

Lucy threw back the duvet, caught her foot in the crumpled cover and tumbled out of bed, spilling coffee all over her, and the bed.

It was clearly going to be one of those days.

Mopping up as best she could with a handful of tissues, she yanked off the sopping bedding and threw it in a heap on the floor, jumping over it to get to the shower. In less than twenty minutes she was ready, having simply towel-dried, her long, thick hair. At least one good thing had resulted from her sunburn: she required no foundation or blusher to add colour to her complexion.

She applied lipstick and mascara and almost fell down stairs in her haste to get to the kitchen and a cup of coffee she could drink, rather than throw all over her. She needed caffeine before she came face-to-face with Evan.

'Wow!' Evan said, as she and Beatrix stepped out into the sunshine. 'You look different from the last time I saw you. Although the lobster effect was fetching, the tan suits you better.'

She returned his smile. 'Where have you been for the last couple of days? Not that I've missed you or anything. I was merely surprised not to bump into you in such a small place as this.'

And now she was babbling like an idiot. Great.

'That's a pity,' he said, looking her directly in the eye. 'Because I've missed you. I've been thinking about what you said. The bit about me believing I want Diana, but life telling me I don't need her.'

Lucy waited for him to continue, but he didn't. What did he mean by that? Was he saying that he was finally getting over Diana? Well, it was about time. Or was he saying that he still loved her but had realised he could get on with his life and live without her?

Did it matter? Lucy would like to say it didn't, but the plain truth was, it did. It mattered very much.

Evan hardly got to say another word, and neither did Lucy. During the time it took the three of them to walk from the cottages to The Coffee Hideaway, Beatrix chatted constantly about her hopes for meeting Jamie McDay. She asked what she should say to him, but didn't wait for their answer. Instead she ran through possible scenarios, acting the parts of both herself and Jamie as if performing a private play for Lucy and Evan.

Lucy was more than a little relieved when they finally reached the red painted door of the welcoming café. Heavenly aromas of bacon and eggs drifted towards her as Evan opened the door and held it for Lucy and Beatrix to enter.

'I think I know what I'm having,' Lucy said, as they joined the end of the small queue of four people. She was already salivating at the prospect of a cooked breakfast and copious amounts of freshly brewed coffee.

'He's not here.' Beatrix sounded disappointed.

'Did you really expect him to be?' Evan asked. 'Didn't Holly say that he and Laurel were coming home today? It's only eight-fifteen. Why don't you ask Trixie what time they're expected?'

'Shush! Because I didn't want to make it obvious that I'm here to see Jamie. If I ask Trixie, she's bound to tell them I've been waiting for him or something. You know what she's like. Or maybe you don't. Anyway, I wanted it to seem as if it was a pure coincidence and that I just happened to be here having coffee when they arrived.'

He shook his head at Beatrix, and grinned at Lucy. 'Is the plan to stay here all day then? What if they don't get back until this evening?'

Lucy shrugged. 'I think Holly said they'd be back this morning.'

'I suppose that narrows it down to before noon,' Evan said. 'Assuming they're not delayed, of course. If they have been, I'm sure they'll have let Trixie know.'

The thought of spending the entire day in The Coffee Hideaway did not appeal to Lucy, especially in thirty plus degree heat, and only partial air conditioning.

'Hello, Trixie,' she said when they reached the front of

the queue a short while later. 'What time are you expecting Laurel to be back? I'm really looking forward to meeting her.'

Evan chuckled and Beatrix glowered but Trixie fanned herself with the menu and leant back against the shelf behind her.

'Anytime now, I hope. My darling girl said they'd be home for breakfast. I love helping out here, don't get me wrong, but it's been like Piccadilly Circus this morning and everyone wants cooked breakfast. I could do with a sit-down and a cup of tea. What can I get you?'

'Er.' Lucy gave Trixie her sweetest smile. 'I almost hate to ask, but I'd love a cooked breakfast.'

'Me too,' Beatrix said, glancing over her shoulder towards the door.

'Just toast and coffee for me, please,' Evan added.

'Right you are.' Trixie smiled, in spite of the additional breakfasts. 'Take a seat and I'll get them to you as fast as I can.'

'Oh, there's no rush, Trixie,' Beatrix said. 'We don't have any plans today so take your time. It's far too hot to be dashing about. Why don't you have that cup of tea? '

'Well, that's very thoughtful of you, dear.' Trixie rewarded Beatrix with a huge smile. 'But as I was always telling my darling Laurel, the customers always come first. And just because my daughter owns the place, that doesn't give me the right to take liberties.'

'Whatever you say, Trixie.' Beatrix smiled and headed for the table closest to the door. 'I'll be able to see them coming, from here,' she said to Lucy.

'Oh good.' Lucy sat down beside her and Evan sat opposite. 'Unless they come from the opposite direction. Keep your eyes peeled, Evan. We don't want to miss them among the crowd. We've already seen four other people

86

this morning.'

Beatrix didn't respond to Lucy's sarcasm. She was far too busy staring out the window.

Chapter Twelve

'Jamie McDay looks even better in real life than he does in the movies,' Lucy said as she watched him walk towards them, half an hour later. He was arm in arm with Laurel, on the opposite side of Market Street and neither of them seemed in a hurry. 'I'd assumed that Hollywood make-up artists had the skills to improve a person's appearance, not make them less attractive.'

'Ah yes,' Evan commented, twisting in his seat to get a better view. 'But he does play the part of a vampire in that phenomenally successful film trilogy. I can't remember what it's called.'

'It's not called that,' Lucy joked. 'It's called, *Keep A Lid On It* – the *It* being Jamie's character, Adam.'

'Perhaps he's not meant to be very good looking – as a vampire, I mean.'

'I don't know. He still looks pretty hot to me. For a dead guy.'

'Shush,' Beatrix said. 'He's coming.'

No sooner had he stepped over the threshold, having held the door open for Laurel than Beatrix was on her feet. Lucy yanked her back down.

'Give the man a chance to get inside. He won't thank

you for accosting him the moment he walks through the door. Just wait until they've had time to say hello to Trixie and then go to the counter and order more coffee. That way you can say hello without appearing like the crazed fan you really are.'

'Good idea.' Beatrix perched on the edge of the seat like a sprinter at the block.

'Relax, Beatrix,' Evan advised. 'Lucy's right. You do look a little crazy.'

Beatrix glowered at him. 'I don't think you understand how important this is. He's a Hollywood movie star. I'm a struggling actor. He could give me all sorts of tips. He might even be prepared to put my name forward as an extra in the new film they're making over here. That could open all sorts of doors for me.'

'Then don't you think it's better to wait for the right moment?' Lucy suggested, still hanging onto Beatrix's arm in case she tried to bolt.

'I suppose so.'

Trixie greeted Laurel and Jamie as if she hadn't seen them for years, throwing her arms around them and hugging them close. She even seemed to shed a few tears.

'It's so good to have you back,' she sobbed. 'I've missed you so much.'

'We've missed you too, Mum,' Laurel said. She glanced over Trixie's shoulder as they hugged, and her eyes opened wide. 'Beatrix? Is that you? Sorry, Mum. I just spotted Beatrix.'

'Yes, it's me.' Beatrix sprang to her feet, and Lucy let her go. 'How are you, Laurel?'

'I'm really good, thanks, and I must say you're looking pretty fabulous. You've changed your hair colour, haven't you?'

Trixie wiped her eyes. 'I'll make you coffee. You're

bound to want coffee.'

Jamie smiled at Trixie and gave her a bear hug, lifting her off the ground and spinning her around. 'Make mine a *Laurel*,' he said when he finally set her down.

Laurel gave him a loving glance and took her hand in his. 'I want you to meet a friend of mine, Jamie. This is Beatrix, Petunia's niece.'

Laurel and Jamie walked towards Beatrix but she met them halfway.

'It's so good to meet you,' Beatrix said. 'I'm a huge fan.'

'Thanks. It's great to meet you too.'

'Beatrix is an actor, Jamie,' Laurel said, with evident excitement. 'And have you seen the colour of her hair?'

Jamie's brows knit together for a moment and then he smiled. 'Oh yes. Well! Would you believe it!'

'Er. Am I missing something?' Beatrix looked confused.

'It must be fate,' Laurel enthused. 'We were just talking about it a moment ago. Weren't we, darling?' She beamed at Jamie.

'We were.'

'Sorry. What?' Beatrix glanced over at Lucy and Evan.

Laurel laughed. 'Oh, I'm sorry, Beatrix. You must think we're mad. The thing is, the last time I saw you your hair was brown and I didn't for one minute think about suggesting you dye it. Or even wear a wig. Ginger is one of those colours that doesn't suit everyone.'

'And it's important it looks natural,' Jamie added.

Laurel nodded. 'Exactly. And it does, doesn't it?'

'Definitely,' agreed Jamie. 'But why didn't you mention her?'

'I don't know,' Laurel exclaimed. 'I honestly don't. I should have. Of course I should have.'

'Um. Thanks,' Beatrix said. 'I'm really pleased you like it. My friend Lucy suggested it. Oh, sorry. That's Lucy. That's Evan. But you may already know Evan. He's Bartram's nephew.'

'Yes. I think we met once. Many years ago. It's good to see you again, Evan. Hello, Lucy. It's lovely to meet you.'

'Can we save all the hellos for later?' Jamie said. 'I don't mean to be rude but I have to ask this first. Beatrix, are you working at the moment?'

Beatrix blinked several times. 'Um. Not right now.'

'Would you like to audition for a part in the next *Keep A Lid On It* film? We're looking for someone with exactly that colour hair. I think you would be perfect. Assuming you can act, of course.'

Beatrix's shriek nearly deafened Lucy.

'Oh! She can act,' Lucy said. 'Believe me. I'm not just saying that because I'm her friend. She really can.'

'Then what are you doing tomorrow, Beatrix? Would you have time to audition?'

All Beatrix did was nod.

Lucy sighed. 'She'll have time. And she's not usually like this, I assure you. She's just incredibly excited.'

Jamie grinned and nodded. 'I get that. I've been there. I'm not making any promises, Beatrix. It's all down to you and your performance. Just make sure you can speak by tomorrow.'

'Oh, I'll do more than speak,' Beatrix said, suddenly finding her voice. 'I promise I won't let you down. Thank you so much for this opportunity. You don't know how much this means. I really am a huge fan. I love the films. What time tomorrow? Where? Do you have a copy of the script so that I can practise? Should I—?'

'Calm down, Beatrix.' Jamie patted her on her shoulder. 'We'll be in The Snowdrop Inn this evening.

Meet us for a drink and we'll discuss it later. Okay?'

'Absolutely. See you later. Thank you, thank you both so much.'

Lucy leant across the table towards Evan. 'I don't believe that just happened. Do you?'

Evan leant forward and met her gaze. 'No. But it did. Someone told me... I think it was Janet Gilroy... that anything can happen in Hideaway Down.'

Lucy looked deep into his eyes. 'I think she may be right.'

Evan reached out and brushed a wayward strand of hair from Lucy's face. 'I'm absolutely certain she is.'

Chapter Thirteen

'Cash robbers and thieves.' Nikki's voice rang out on the other end of the line less than two seconds after Lucy pressed 'call'. 'This was Lucy Draycourt's office but as she seems to have disappeared off the face of the earth and hasn't bothered to tell her long-suffering PA whether she has or hasn't been having rampant sex in haystacks for over a week, it no longer is. How may I help you?'

'Firstly, Nikki, it hasn't been over a week and... Oh God, you're right! I haven't called you since last Friday evening, have I?'

'Sorry, to whom am I speaking? I'm afraid I don't recognise your voice.'

'Okay. I'm sorry. Please forgive me. I've lost all track of time. Don't blame me, blame this place. It's as if the former Lucy Draycourt has disappeared and a completely different one has been put in her place. Come on, Nikki. I'll tell you all about Evan. The guy I—'

'I remember who he is. So tell me. How much sex and how many haystacks?'

'Apparently, it's a little too early in the season for haystacks. And unfortunately there hasn't been any sex either but—'

'No sex? What the bloody hell have you been doing all week then?'

'Sleeping and reading for the most part.'

'Do what?' Nikki let out a false hoot of laughter. 'Sorry, I thought you said you'd been sleeping and reading.'

'I did. I can't believe how tired I've been.'

'When you said you've become a completely different person, I didn't realise what you meant was you've turned into an eighty-year-old. You're not serious, are you? Oh. My. God. You are. Get out of there Lucy while you still can.'

'I like it here. It's a little hard to believe, I know, but this place really gets under your skin.'

'So does bacteria. Get out now! It's that accident you had last Friday, isn't it? You're suffering from the after effects of being knocked over, aren't you? You've got brain damage or something.'

'I'm absolutely fine. In fact, I'm better than fine. I'm having a lovely time. Well, I would be if I could understand what's going on in Evan Foster's gorgeous mind. I think it's very possible that I've fallen in love.'

'Okay, that's it. I'm calling the paramedics. And the SAS. And MI5 and whoever else I can think of. What about Henry? Have you forgotten about him?'

'Almost entirely, I'm sorry to say. No. I'm happy to say that. Henry's much too old for me.'

'Not to mention the fact that the guy's a boring old fart with about as much passion in him as a post-it-note.'

'Post-it-notes can be very passionate. You can write little love notes on them and stuff like that. And you seem to have forgotten that Henry did kiss me in the lift last month.'

'Yeah, but only because we spiked his drink. And even then all he did was kiss you.'

'You spiked his drink? You didn't tell me that.'

'Oops.'

'Nikki! So you're saying that the only reason he kissed me was because he was drunk? No wonder he never mentioned it again.'

'We didn't know he'd kiss you. We only did it for a laugh and because he's such a pompous prat. I think he kissed you because he does actually like you. He's just so far up his own backside that he doesn't know how to ask you out.'

'Well. He's missed his chance.'

'So... this Evan guy? Are you saying that once again you've fallen for someone who is showing no interest whatsoever in you?'

'Yes. Well, no. Not exactly. That's the problem. One minute he does seem interested. I'd even go as far as to say, very interested. The next, he's avoiding me like I'm one of the walking dead. He thinks he's still in love with his ex-fiancée who dumped him two years ago and ran off with his best friend and business partner.'

'What? His fiancée ran off with two people?'

'Don't be pedantic. You know what I mean.'

'Do me a favour, Lucy. Fall in love with someone normal, will you? Why is your love life always so complicated?'

'Isn't love always complicated?'

'No. You meet someone you like. They like you. You date, you kiss, you have great sex, you fall in love, get married, get divorced, get drunk. Rinse and repeat.'

'Hmm. What happened to living happily ever after?'

'It's the curse of the modern age. No one lives happily ever after these days.'

'I don't believe that.'

'Says the girl who's in love with a guy who's in love with his ex who's in love with his friend. Have you kissed him?'

'Yes. But I was drunk so I can't actually remember it. I woke up naked in his bed so we—'

'Whoa! You did what now? I thought you said you hadn't had sex.'

'I haven't. We didn't. We were both too drunk.'

'This gets worse. So you're naked in his bed. Then what?'

'Nothing. Well, not much anyway. We've chatted quite a bit and he rubbed after-sun all over me when I got burnt.'

'He what? Excuse me for saying this, Lucy, but you're a weirdo. You do know that, right? You're telling me you've been naked or semi-naked or a little bit naked more than once but you haven't had sex or even kissed him other than when you were both drunk?'

'Yes. That's why I'm calling. I need some advice.'

'You need more than advice, Lucy. You need psychiatric help. But I'll see what I can do.'

'Okay. Just one simple question. If you like a guy and you're pretty sure he likes you but he doesn't want to admit it because he thinks he's still in love with someone else, do you tell him? Or do you just grab him and kiss him and see what happens?'

'That's two questions. And why aren't you asking Beatrix?'

'I have. I want a second opinion.'

'Why? Didn't you like the first? What did she say?'

'She said to go for it. Ooh, I forgot to tell you. Beatrix has a boyfriend – and he's a really great guy. And... You know that famous actor, Jamie McDay? Well, we've met him, and yesterday, Beatrix auditioned for a part in his new film. And she got it! It's quite a big part, so she's finally going to be a film star. Isn't that absolutely fabulous?'

'Absolutely. Say congrats for me. She must be thrilled. It's all happening in Hideaway Down by the sound of it.'

'That's the understatement of the year. And Beatrix is going crazy with excitement. I'm so happy that things are finally working out for her.'

'So back to you. I agree with Beatrix. Go for it. When are you planning to do this? You've only got tonight and the wedding's tomorrow, isn't it? You're leaving on Sunday, aren't you?'

'That's the plan. It can't be tonight though because Evan and the guys are going out for dinner and Evan's got to help Bartram get ready tomorrow. He's Bartram's nephew and also the best man.'

'Really? So that just leaves tomorrow. You'll have to do it at the reception. But make sure neither of you gets drunk this time. And I'd do it all. I'd grab him, kiss him and then tell him how I feel, because if there's one thing I know for sure about a lot of men, it's that they're pretty bloody stupid when it comes to reading signals.'

Chapter Fourteen

Petunia Welsley looked stunning in a simple, fitted gown of ivory silk. She had personally hand-embroidered the bodice with row upon row of the symbol for infinity.

Ivy said that she thought they were meant to be a string of sausages as a little 'nod' to the fact that Bartram owned the village butchers, and his handmade sausages were a speciality.

'I think it's romantic,' she said. 'I'd be happy to have horseshoes embroidered on my wedding dress to acknowledge the fact that Ned's a blacksmith.'

'And that you're an old nag,' Holly added.

Lucy wished Ivy hadn't mentioned sausages. Apart from the fact that she had skipped breakfast due to nerves about her plan to tell Evan how she felt about him, every time she looked at Petunia after Ivy's comment, all she could see was sausages.

Evan was once again ignoring her. Why couldn't the man make up his mind? He either liked her or he didn't. Was that so difficult? And she was beginning to lose patience with the whole 'Diana thing'. If the woman was going to come back, she'd have done so long before now. Wasn't it time he accepted that and got on with his life?

Even if he didn't want Lucy in it – although she rather hoped he would.

Beatrix and Harry couldn't keep their eyes – or their hands off one another and Beatrix hadn't stopped smiling since the minute Jamie had told her she had got the part in his film, so she walked down the aisle beaming from ear to ear. Some people may have thought it was because she had to walk behind the Gaggle Gang who behaved better than some of the guests – and were even better dressed in their lavender bow ties and tiny top hats held in place by lavender coloured silk ribbons.

Beatrix's parents, Petunia's older brother, Michael and his wife, Thelma had arrived late due to heavy traffic. Michael was giving Petunia away so it had all been a little manic before the ceremony, with text messages flying back and forth and phones constantly beeping, like new-age wedding music. As they walked down the aisle, Thelma kept waving frantically and smiling like a lunatic.

Holly and Ivy followed Beatrix; Laurel and Lucy followed them, with Petunia and Michael at the rear.

Bartram and Evan watched their approach; Evan was smiling and avoiding Lucy's eyes, whilst Bartram, close to tears, gripped Evan's arm as if he might fall at any moment from sheer excitement.

Kev the Rev wore white and gold vestments but he'd previously shown Petunia and her entourage that beneath his formal garments he wore white trousers and a gold T-shirt with the words, *Petunia and Bartram, Together Forever*, emblazoned in white glitter across the front. This was Lucy's first experience of the Reverend, and until Beatrix explained that he was harmless and merely liked to enjoy life, she wondered whether there had been a big mistake and the man had escaped from a local establishment for the mentally impaired.

The ceremony went off without a hitch, although when Kev the Rev had asked if anyone had reason to object, Bartram had looked extremely anxious as if he believed there may be a possibility that someone might. He had repeatedly told everyone in The Snowdrop Inn the night before that he hoped and prayed Petunia wouldn't change her mind and realise she could do much better.

After the ceremony, Evan continued to avoid Lucy as everyone except the bride and groom who were in a lavish, flower-strewn horse and carriage, made their way on foot down Market Street to The Snowdrop Inn. Once more, the Gaggle Gang led the way.

Speeches were made, toasts were proposed and the cake, a beautiful three-tier confection of marbled sponge covered in white chocolate icing and strawberries, was cut. People mingled, presents were opened and several bottles of champagne, wine and beer were consumed.

But still Evan avoided Lucy. This was getting ridiculous. Something had to be done – and soon, or she might miss her chance and tomorrow they would go their separate ways. The thought of not seeing him again gave Lucy palpitations.

'We're going to the fair,' Beatrix announced, 'and if you're looking for Evan – which I know you are so don't pretend you're not – Harry's already asked him and he's coming too.'

Chapter Fifteen

The August Fair was not as Lucy had imagined. She had expected it to be made up of fast rides and flashing lights and over-priced 'tag-a-duck' stalls or such, with tacky prizes. Instead, it consisted of tall, elegant, tent-like emporiums, the entrances spread open to reveal all manner of goods, from beautiful, handmade cushions, to expertly carved wooden ornaments. There were tents with homemade cakes and tents where people performed skilled crafts, giving tutorials to paying customers, and the only rides, neither of which were fast, were an old-fashioned Ferris Wheel and a colourful Carousel.

'Not what you expected, Lucy?' Harry asked.

Lucy shook her head. 'No. It's like stepping back in time.'

'It's more of a craft fair than a funfair,' Beatrix said. 'Jarvis Pope, the head of The Hideaway Cliff Preservation Trust is also one of the organisers of the fair, and he won't allow any of the modern, flashy rides. He says, "If the young people want that kind of thing, they can go to Eastbourne." Sorry, I can't mimic his voice very well, but you get the picture.'

'I think I like this Jarvis Pope,' Lucy replied. 'I

definitely like this fair!'

'Look!' Beatrix pointed to one tent in particular, the entrance of which was closed. 'There's a fortune teller there. Let's see what the future has in store for all of us. C'mon.' She dashed towards it, pulling Harry along with her.

'Hmm. I'm not sure I want to know. How about you?' She glanced at Evan who was walking beside her although he hadn't said one word to her all day and that hadn't changed since they'd left The Snowdrop Inn.

He shrugged. 'I don't believe in the whole fortune telling bit, so I'm not really interested. I can tell your future though. I think you're leaning towards throwing away good money to be told a lot of rubbish.'

Lucy grinned. 'I'll wait and see what *Skylar Lake* tells Beatrix and Harry,' she said, reading the name, written on an A-board, in a ghost-like hand over an image of a crystal ball. 'Do you think that's her real name?'

Evan grinned back. 'I don't doubt it for a minute.'

'I'm going in,' Beatrix said, taking a deep breath and sticking out her chest.

'She's a fortune teller, Beatrix, you're not going into battle. Relax.' Harry kissed her on the cheek. 'D'you want me to go first?'

'No. Maybe. I don't know.'

'Why don't you ask Skylar Lake who should go first?' Evan said.

Beatrix frowned. 'Don't be sarcastic. I'm actually a bit nervous.'

'Then don't do it,' suggested Evan. 'No one's forcing you.'

She shook her head. 'I know but... I sort of feel... compelled.'

'Oooh,' Harry said. 'Perhaps she's using mind control.

You know. Like those hypnotists do on TV.'

Evan smiled. 'Yes. That must be it. You *will* have your fortune told, Beatrix, and when I snap my fingers you'll hand over all your money.'

'Ha, ha.' Beatrix pulled a face. 'Right, that's it. I'm going.'

'Come in,' an eerie voice called from inside the tent, making them all jump.

'She knows we're here!' Beatrix whispered, her eyes as big as saucers.

Evan leant forward and lowered his voice: 'Of course she does, Beatrix. The tent's made from material. She can hear us.' He gave a little laugh.

Beatrix straightened up, tutted, and went inside.

Lucy, Evan and Harry exchanged doubtful glances.

'I wonder how long it'll take,' Lucy said.

'The board says £15 for 15 minutes.' Evan nodded towards it. 'I suppose we can safely say that's how long it'll take. Of course, she could speak really slowly so that her punters have to pay another £15 to actually find out anything.'

Harry laughed. 'What? Like, "and you'll meet... Oh sorry, we've run out of time". She could keep doing that until Beatrix runs out of money.'

Lucy nodded. 'And knowing Beatrix, she'll pay it.' Although after all the fabulous things that had happened for Beatrix this week, Lucy wondered what else the future had in store for her friend.

'Let's get an ice cream while we wait,' Evan suggested, nodding towards a tent opposite where a generator buzzed like a swarm of bees and tubs of colourful ice cream promised cold refreshment and relief from the heat of the afternoon sun.

103

Chapter Sixteen

'So what did she say?' Lucy asked the second Beatrix's head popped out from Skylar Lake's tent.

'You look very pleased,' Harry said, 'so it must have been good things.'

Beatrix nodded. 'She's incredible.' She lowered her voice as if she didn't want the fortune teller to hear. 'She knew everything about me. She said that I'd very recently met two very different men who would both help to shape my future. One with bushy red hair and one very dark-haired! Can you believe that? It's you, Harry. You... and Jamie McDay. How could she possibly have known that?'

'What else did she say about me?' Harry looked a little worried.

Beatrix blushed. 'I'm not sure I should tell you. I don't want to jinx it.'

'How could you jinx it?' Lucy wanted to know what Beatrix had been told. If Skylar Lake was that good about the past, perhaps she could tell Lucy something about hers. 'Did she say anything else about your past, or just what's happened this week?'

'She said I live in a city with a friend, but that's going to change and that I'm about to embark on a new adventure which will bring me everything I've ever wanted. She saw my picture on a billboard and bright lights in my future but said my feet were firmly rooted in the ground so I wouldn't get swept away.'

'Wow,' Harry said, but there was an edge to his voice.

'So does that mean you'll be moving out?' Lucy felt as if the world had been taken from under her. For some reason, she hadn't considered the possibility of Beatrix leaving the flat they shared. Of moving on.

Beatrix took her hand. 'I don't know. I... I hadn't thought about what that meant. I suppose it might. But it won't change things between us, Lucy. We've been best friends since Uni and we'll be best friends forever.'

'Of course we will.'

That was true, Lucy knew that much. And she wanted whatever was best for Beatrix. She wanted her friend to be happy. If that meant Beatrix moving out, then Lucy would just have to get used to the idea. Harry didn't look quite so sure.

'Aren't they filming in Sussex?' Evan asked. 'The Vampire movie, I mean. I'm sure Jamie said last night that the property scouts had found an old mansion just a few miles from Hideaway Down and that it was perfect for the film. One of his stipulations was that he wants to be able to live here and travel to the shoot each day, so I don't think you'll be going far for a while, Beatrix.'

'I like the sound of that.' Harry visibly brightened.

'You should have yours done, Harry,' Beatrix suggested.

'I think I will. Do you mind if I go next, Lucy?'

Lucy shook her head. 'Not at all. It'll be interesting to see what she says about you.

Harry gave a nervous smile and dashed into the tent.

Beatrix beamed at Lucy and Evan. 'She also said I'd

have three children, all with red bushy hair, but I didn't think I should mention that to Harry just yet.'

Evan coughed as if something had caught in his throat, but Lucy couldn't have been happier.

'Oh Beatrix, that's wonderful!' She threw her arms around Beatrix and hugged her tightly. 'You'd better make me a godmother or there'll be trouble.'

Beatrix laughed. 'Don't worry, Lucy, you will be. And I know you'll be their favourite aunt. I'm already thinking about their names.'

'Dear God!' Evan said. 'I think Harry will need a very large drink if she tells him what she's told you.'

Something flashed across Beatrix's eyes.

'You do think she meant that I'm going to end up with Harry, don't you? That the kids with bushy red hair are his?'

'Of course,' Lucy said. 'Who else could she have meant?'

Beatrix still looked anxious. 'Well, I suppose there could be other men with bushy red hair but I just assumed she meant Harry when she told me that. What if she tells him something completely different?'

'I'd be surprised if she did.' Evan said.

'You believe in it then?' Beatrix asked.

Evan shrugged. 'She seems to have got a few things right about you but she could have heard people talking in the village or even seen you in the pub or something. The point is, you've just been in to see her and she's told you about a guy with red hair. You come out and a guy with red hair goes in. You don't need to be a fortune teller to know that you're probably together.'

'Cynic,' Lucy said.

'Realistic,' Evan replied.

'So what will you have to say if she's spot on about

you?'

'I won't be going in, so I won't be saying anything.'

'Really? Isn't this your chance to find out once and for all if…' Lucy stopped mid-sentence. She hadn't meant to say that. The last thing she wanted Evan to be thinking about right now was whether there was a chance that Diana might be coming back.

He narrowed his eyes and frowned for just a second. 'No.'

'Harry!' Beatrix said. 'That was quick. What did she tell you?'

Harry looked a little shell-shocked as he exited the tent but he smiled at Beatrix. He stood there looking at her, his smile growing wider.

'The fortune teller looked surprised when I walked in but she smiled and said: "I don't think I need to tell you what the future has in store for you. She's just been in here."'

Beatrix beamed at him.

'Was that it?' Lucy asked, trying not to glance in Evan's direction.

Harry shook his head. 'No. She told me that I would have opportunities to travel but my responsibilities would always bring me back here, and I wasn't to see that as a bad thing. She said that sometimes life knows what is best for us even if we can't see it at the time.'

'That doesn't sound good,' Beatrix said. She sounded disappointed.

'I think that just means you won't be living in Hollywood,' Lucy said, trying to reassure her.

'Oh,' Beatrix said.

Harry nodded. 'She told me that I'd have a very happy marriage… and three children. I think I like the sound of that.'

That had made Beatrix happier. 'She said the same to me!'

Harry and Beatrix stared lovingly into each other's eyes, neither quite sure about what to do next it seemed.

'Right,' Lucy said. 'I think it's my turn. But I'm feeling a little nervous.'

'Oh don't be,' Beatrix assured her. 'She's really nice and she puts you at ease immediately. Doesn't she, Harry?'

Harry nodded, still staring at Beatrix.

'Okay then.' Lucy shot a quick glance at Evan, who hadn't said a word since her comment, which he had obviously realised was about Diana. He was looking at her intently, as if he had something very important on his mind.

Chapter Seventeen

'Hello,' Lucy said, as she walked into the dimly-lit tent. 'So how does this work? Do I just sit down and listen?'

Skylar's head shot up and she stared at Lucy as if she'd seen a ghost. Her face drained of colour and her fingers clenched the edge of the table where she was sitting.

'Oh my God!' Lucy said, grabbing the back of the chair she'd been about to sit on. 'You've seen something bad, haven't you?'

Skylar blinked several times. 'Luciana?' she finally said, her voice cracking with emotion. 'Is it really you?'

Okay, that was really spooky. The woman had used Lucy's birth name and not many people knew that. Although she had pronounced it differently. With a hint of a foreign accent about it. Italian sprang to mind.

'Wow!' Lucy said, managing to walk around the chair and sit down even though her legs were suddenly shaking. 'You really are good. Can you tell me anything about my parents? About why they gave me up?'

Skylar reached out and took both of Lucy's hands, squeezing them tightly. She shook her head and there were clearly tears in her eyes as she did so.

'Your parents didn't give you up, Luciana. They loved

you very much.'

'Really? Then why did they abandon me outside a church?'

'They didn't.' Skylar let go of one of Lucy's hands and wiped the tears which were now rolling down her cheeks. 'They didn't abandon you. I was the one who left you outside the church.'

What did she just say?

'I wanted to keep you with me, but I was only sixteen and we weren't related, so there was no way the authorities would have let me.'

'What?' Lucy couldn't believe what she was hearing. 'What are you talking about? Are you seeing someone doing this or are you...are you saying that this really happened? That...that you actually *know* me?'

Skylar nodded. 'It actually happened. I certainly know you, Luciana. Well I did, many, many years ago. I think I should explain.'

'Yes,' Lucy snapped. 'I definitely think you should.'

Skylar took a long, slow breath. It looked as if she was finding this difficult, which was nothing to how Lucy was feeling.

'Your mother's name was Aurelia, your father's, Finnian. Finnian Green. And it breaks my heart to tell you this but they died instantly, in a massive, motorway accident on the fifth of September, a few days after your first birthday.'

'Oh my God! Wh-what happened?'

Skylar shook her head and reached back out to retrieve Lucy's other hand.

'We were all on the way to our next fair. It was very early in the morning, and raining heavily. I'm still not sure what happened. I was in the truck two vehicles behind yours. All I remember about that day is the noise and the

110

smell of rubber, as vehicles, one after the other, ploughed into each other. It was a miracle you survived and were completely unscathed when the firemen pulled you from the wreckage. You were wrapped in one of Aurelia's shawls at the time and after you'd been checked over by the paramedics and put in an ambulance, I jumped in with you and waited. It was complete mayhem, as you can imagine.'

'And... you knew my parents were dead? You... you saw them?'

'Yes. Neither of them had any living relatives, so I knew that either the rest of our community would try to get custody of you, or you'd be given up for adoption. As I held you in my arms, surrounded by police and fire crew, I saw a better future for you. So I chose my moment and ran off with you, up the bank of the motorway and went to the town on the other side. I caught a train and left you outside the church I had seen in my vision. Afterwards, I went to the hospital I'd heard the paramedics mention, and I told the survivors of our troupe what I'd done. There were so many injured that none of the authorities noticed you'd gone, and there was no record of you, so we all kept quiet... and life went on. I kept telling myself I would go back and find you one day. Tell you what happened. Tell you about your parents. But my visions told me not to. That you were happy. That you were loved and cherished. And that, when you were ready and the time was right, you would find me. And here we are.'

'I... I don't know what to say.'

'This must be an even bigger shock to you than it is to me. I knew I would see you again – and I have been thinking about you a lot lately, but I hadn't foreseen this meeting. It seems the Universe wanted it to be a surprise for me as well as for you. I'm sure you've been happy but

I'd like to hear it from you. I'd like to be absolutely certain that I did the right thing that day.'

Lucy nodded. 'I've been very happy. Very happy indeed. I couldn't have wanted better parents. But... it would have been nice to know that my birth parents hadn't abandoned me. That they loved me and hadn't given me away. It would... it would've been... comforting, in a way, to know that the reason I wasn't with them was only because they were dead.'

Skylar smiled wanly. 'I thought about that sometime later. I should've put that in the note. But I'd written it hastily on the train. A teenager opposite me left her pad and pen on the table when she nipped to the loo. I stole a page and scribbled the note before she came back. I just wrote what came into my head. I think I was still in a state of shock myself and wasn't thinking clearly. I'm sorry.'

'No. Please don't apologise. It's a lot to take in, but I think you did what you thought was best for me.'

'I did what I believe Aurelia told me to do. I believe she sent me that vision before she passed over. She sent me to a place I'd never even heard of, but she knew it was where you'd find the love you'd need. The love of a family. The love she was no longer able to give you herself. I honestly believe that, Luciana.'

'I... I go by the name of Lucy, now. My parents... my adoptive parents, shortened it to that. But why Luciana? I mean... why was I named Luciana? And is that how it's pronounced? Loo-chee-ana? We all thought it was pronounced Lucy-anna.'

Skylar shook her head vigorously 'Ah. No. It's Italian. I don't know why but both Aurelia and Finnian loved all things Italian. They went to Italy for their honeymoon, I know that. They spent it with a group of Italian Romanies. That's where the original Romani, or Roma people come from. From Italy. But Aurelia would be happy with the name of Lucy. It's a pretty name and not far removed from Luciana – which means *Light* by the way. They both said you were the light of their lives, so perhaps that's why they chose the name.'

'That's... that's beautiful.' Lucy struggled to hold back the tears pricking at her eyes. 'Do you... do you have any photos of them? Of my parents?'

'No. I'm so sorry, but I don't. You are the image of Aurelia though – and you have Finnian's eyes. It's as if both Aurelia and Finnian are here with me now, just looking at you. They were wonderful, kind and gentle people. I still miss them. I think I always shall. Be happy, Luciana. Live your life to the full. Do what you want to, not what you think you should. Your adoptive parents will love you no matter what. And... I see you laughing, surrounded by fields of lavender and poppies, with a blond man, who is kind and who loves you more than he thought possible. I see you... in Italy. In Italy, Luciana. Perhaps on your honeymoon too.' Skylar let out a long, slow breath and smiled lovingly. 'You will live a long and very happy life, Luciana. I can see it.'

'Thank you.' Lucy didn't know what to say. After everything Skylar had told her, was that the fortune telling bit? Had she reverted to her calling? Lucy reached for her purse to pay her.

'What are you doing, Luciana?' Skylar seemed genuinely shocked. 'You think I want you to pay me? I can't believe it.'

'Sorry I... I...' Tears fell from her eyes and she couldn't stop them.

Skylar jumped to her feet and pulled her close, hugging her tightly. 'Don't cry, Luciana. I didn't mean to shout at you. It is all such a shock. I know. Go to your friends.

Speak to your adoptive parents. I shall be here and if you want to come and talk to me some more, you are always welcome. You will always be welcome. You are one of us. I shall give you my mobile number. Call me at any time. Any time, Luciana. I mean this.'

Lucy sniffed and wiped her eyes. 'Thank you, Skylar. Thank you. And I don't mean just for this. For today. I mean for everything. For what you did for me. For what you did for my parents. Thank you.'

Skylar nodded and brushed her hand across her eyes. 'Now go, Luciana. Before I am in a flood of tears. Go and be happy. And keep in touch.'

'I shall, Skylar. I definitely shall.'

Lucy blinked away her tears, and with a final smile for the woman who had, in so many ways, given Lucy her life back, she stepped out into the sunshine with a blissful smile on her face.

'Wow!' Beatrix said. 'She must have told you you're going to have a wonderful future. You were in there for ages and you look as if you know you're going to win the lottery or something. Is that what she told you?'

'She told me something far, far better than that, Beatrix. She told me about my past. She told me about my parents.'

Evan took her hand. 'Are you okay, Lucy? You look to me as if you've been crying. Come with me and we'll find somewhere to sit down.'

Lucy beamed at him. 'I have, Evan, but I'm fine. Honestly. I don't need to sit down. In fact, Evan, what I really want to do is to kiss you. Right here, right now. Would that be okay with you?'

'What?' she heard Beatrix exclaim. She also heard Harry give a little, embarrassed cough.

But Evan said nothing. He merely stood and stared at

114

her for what seemed like several minutes but in reality was just a few seconds. Then he took a deep breath, cocked his head to one side and smiled.

'Does this mean you're going to try to seduce me again? Because if it does, let me tell you now, Lucy Draycourt...' He pulled her into his arms, slid one hand into her hair and gently tipped her head back so that she was looking directly into his eyes. 'You'd better be thinking seriously about having a long-term relationship with me. I'm really not into one- night stands. Okay?'

He kissed her so passionately that she almost did need to sit down by the time he relaxed his hold.

'Okay, Evan,' she said, staring into his eyes. 'I'm fairly certain I can agree to that. In fact. I'm absolutely sure I can.'

He kissed her again.

'Get a room you two,' Beatrix said.

'I don't think they're listening,' said Harry.

This time it was Lucy who eased away from Evan.

'Erm. Have you ever been to Italy?' she asked.

'No,' he said, pulling her back to him.

'Do you want to go?'

'Right now?'

'No, of course not. Not right now. But soon, perhaps?'

'Sounds good to me. I've always wanted to go to Rome. Shall we start there?'

'That sounds perfect.'

He leant in to kiss her again but stopped.

'What about your work? You'd have to take time off. I thought you didn't like doing that.'

'It seems I do,' she said. 'It seems I like it a lot. In fact, I'm thinking of taking a sabbatical. I think a few months off would do me good. What do you think?'

'I think that sounds perfect. In fact, Lucy Draycourt, I

think *you're* perfect.'

'I think you're pretty perfect, too, Evan Foster.'

And when she kissed him again, she knew exactly just how perfect they were for each other. She also knew that Skylar Lake was the genuine article: a fortune teller who could accurately predict the future as well as knowing about the past. And Lucy knew her future was going to be pretty damned perfect. She didn't need Skylar Lake to tell her that.

Thank you

Thank you for reading, *Walking on Sunshine*. I hope you enjoyed it and if so, I would absolutely love it if you would consider telling your friends and/or posting a short review on Amazon. Word of mouth is an author's best friend and very much appreciated. Thanks so much.

COMING SOON

Dancing in the Rain
A Hideaway Down Novel (Book 4)

Happiness comes when you least expect it

When Rachel Simpson's boyfriend, Drew, suggested they should take a break, she thought he meant together, so she rented a holiday cottage in the picturesque village of Hideaway Down for the perfect, autumn getaway surprise. Except she was the one who got the surprise, and now she is spending a week alone in a cottage by the sea. Not quite the fun, romantic break she was hoping for.

Lucas Webb needs to get his act together – or so his friends keep telling him. He's been like a bear with a sore head since his girlfriend dumped him... and that was several months ago. Perhaps a change of scene is what he needs. At least he still has Monty, his beloved dog... and a break by the sea will probably do them both some good.

Is it simply bad luck that this is one of the wettest, windiest autumn weeks since records began? Or does the universe work in mysterious ways?

To see details of my other books, please go to the books page on my website or scan the QR code, below. http://www.emilyharvale.com/books.

***

Scan the code above to see Emily's books on Amazon

To read about me, my books, my work in progress and competitions, freebies, or to contact me, pop over to my website http://www.emilyharvale.com. To be the first to hear about new releases and other news, you can subscribe to my Readers' Club newsletter via the 'Sign me up' box. Or why not come and say 'Hello' on Facebook, Twitter, Instagram or Pinterest. Hope to chat with you soon.

Printed in Great Britain
by Amazon